HE NEVER CAME BACK

Published by BooxAi
ISBN: 978-965-578-297-4

HE NEVER CAME BACK

ERNEST STEWART

CONTENTS

THE WEE FOLK

His name was Albert Higglemier Esq, and Herr Higglemier was half of the Higglemier and Richter law firm, well-known lawyers of Strasbourg. Herr Higglemier had recently acquired a chalet through tax foreclosure in the Black Forrest just outside of Bad Peterstal for a song. With the heat of late June, he decided to spend a few weeks there in the peace and quiet of the deep, dark forest. After the cities heat and the hustle and bustle, he looked forward to getting away as he had with his parents every summer of his youth, so off to the woods he went.

Herr Higglemier headed east in a new Porsche Macan Turbo that he had bought for the trip as, somehow, his Mercedes seemed out of place in the deep woods. And deep woods they were, he thought as he headed south away from Bad Peterstal. He came upon his turn about 20 minutes later and followed a curving road down a long driveway until he came onto a clearing in the thick woods where sat the chalet. He parked the Porsche at the top of the circular driveway and stared at his beautiful chalet.

Herr Higglemier couldn't believe his eyes; the property had looked like a good buy on the internet, but now that he was here, it looked like a great buy how he had obtained it for such a low price had him amazed. He walked around the house before he went inside, and it all looked Wunderbar!

He thought that must be terrible on the inside and prepared himself for the worst as he opened the front door. However, the inside was as beautiful as the outside was. He was prepared to spend $50,000 to fix the place up but from what he could see, he would not have to spend a single Euro cent!

He had bought the property for back taxes the former owner apparently had driven away one day and never came back, his loss was my gain, thought Herr Higglemier. The house was completely furnished, and he went from room to room and looked into the closets. He found that they were still full of clothes, coats, shoes, towels, blankets, and such, even his suitcases were still there! Herr Higglemier didn't know what to make of that, but since it had been a long drive from the city, and he was tired. He decided to unpack his car and try to get settled in and relax.

Half an hour later, his living room was full of his luggage, boxes, and bags and bags of groceries in his kitchen. He put the groceries away first, but again the shelves were full of canned goods, and his freezer full of frozen food but the refrigerator was full of spoiled food, which he quickly threw out and then sprayed the refrigerator with a can of germ killer he had found under the sink. He put away his few groceries once the smell had died down. Why would the former owner take off and leave everything behind, he wondered, and if there was one thing Herr Higglemier loved, it was a good mystery!

He popped a dinner into the microwave as he popped a bottle of champagne to celebrate his good fortune. He poured almost half of the bottle of Bollinger Grand Annee into a large water glass and drank it down; how he needed that to quench his thirst. He refilled the glass and then drank the rest of the bottle and put it in the garbage can and wondered how to dispose of it, or at least how to get it out of the kitchen. He found a pair of steel garbage cans outside the back door and put the foul kitchen bags inside one of them.

He then returned to the kitchen and retrieved his dinner from the microwave and his glass from the table and made his way into the living room. He took a seat on the couch placed the glass and dinner on the coffee table, and tried to turn on a nearby lamp but couldn't find the switch, but by accident found out that all he needed to do was to touch the base. Just in time, too, as the sun was beginning to set.

He found the flat-screen controller and tried to turn on the TV, but the batteries were dead. He had brought his laptop and decided to play a couple of old Beat Club disks, and he suddenly returned to the days of his youth as he had grown up watching Beat Club, and before he had watched the second disk, he had fallen fast asleep on the couch.

He awoke to a stiff neck and bright sunshine pouring through the windows. His head was a bit hung over from the bottle of Bollinger, but after a second cup of expresso, he felt much better and decided to put his clothes and such away. He spent the morning changing sheets and moving the former owners' clothes and stuff in general to a spare guest bedroom down the hall from the master-suite.

By the time it was done, it was noon, and he decided to go to town for more groceries, spare batteries, and find out what were the cable companies, the day of garbage pickup, etc. He stopped at the police station to find out what he could about the former owner. All they knew was about a year ago, they were notified by Deutsche Post that the mailbox was overflowing, and there were at least three months of mail in the mailbox. He learned that the former owner was Ernst Schneider, who was a retired banker from Düsseldorf. He asked whether Herr Schneider had any personal effects and whether he had any family to whom he could send them. No, like Albert, Ernst had never married, so he could keep them or throw them away as he liked. When he bought the property, everything on it was his.

On his first stop home, he stopped at the mailbox and pulled all the mail out and put it into a spare shopping bag and drove around the house and parked next to a three-car garage and fumbled around looking for the key to the side door and eventually found it and went inside. What he found inside was truly amazing.

What he found sitting next to the door was a new 1939 Mercedes-Benz W31 type G4 staff car, and sitting on the other side of that was an American car, a 1936 Auburn boat-tailed speedster 852, and on the other side of that was a two-year-old Audi Q7. It could be a million Euros worth of cars that were suddenly his. Herr Higglemier was stunned by his good fortune. He had paid $25,000 in back taxes, the house alone was worth 20 times that, and now the cars. Truly the gods were smiling down on him!

He decided, for the time being, the Porsche would have to live outdoors as he carefully locked the garage door, then began unloading the car and opened the back door of the house and went in. He put his bags down on the table and then turned and locked the back door. He spent the rest of that day and evening putting things away and bagging up the former resident's things in preparation for going to the local dump on the morrow.

One hundred meters back in the woods, many eyes had been watching Albert's every move. About a quarter of the tribe of local dark fairies took copious notes for the tribal council meeting that would soon come when the moon was full. They had literally made a killing of the former resident, taking all his gold and then inviting him out to their village to have him for dinner and not in the nice way either!

Whether or not Albert would join Ernst was up to the fairy King and Queen to decide. It wouldn't do to get the police involved by making it too obvious that there was something going on as a former King and Queen had done by killing a Schutzstaffel Obersturmbannführer and gotten the Gestapo involved like they had those many years ago. The result was that most of the colony had been wiped out with the few survivors running for their lives. No, many lessons were learned of the mistakes that were made, mistakes that would never be repeated again!

They watched Albert's every move until he went to sleep, and then they walked the mile back to their village in the deep, dark woods. As they reached the village, another crew went to take their places to watch over Albert until they were relieved by the first crew just after sunrise. They would keep a 24-hour watch on Albert until the day of the full moon.

Albert, meanwhile, was unaware of his stalkers and went about relaxing and exploring the local villages, sometimes walking down the shaded lanes for miles on end. While he was gone, the dark fairies took advantage of these sojourns to investigate every aspect of Albert's house, garage, and grounds. By the time of June's full moon, they knew everything they needed to know. Since the full moon fell on the summer solstice, there would be much magic in the air. The trouble was, their cousins, the "light fairies," would be all over the place. Indecent creatures that never wore a stitch of clothing, flying around in the all-together for all to see. It was almost more than a dark fairy could stand.

Not to mention, the light fairies were vegans, eating only honey and fruit with nary a bite of meat. I mean, how was it possible to go through life without tasting those incredibly delicious humans? There were other meats, and they would eat them if they had to. Back during the aftermath of the Gestapo raids, there were no humans to be found, and they had to make do with squirrels and hares. Those were bleak days indeed. They moved what was left of their village and what was left of their clan a full twenty miles away from its current location, deeper into the forest.

They had their gardens, but they grew mostly garlic, onions, herbs, and spices, things that would enhance the flavor of the meat. The occasional yam or pumpkin for festivals and celebrations and a score of apple trees for the making of hard cider, their favorite drink.

On the day of the full moon and summer solstice, an old friend of Albert's, Hannah Mueller, called to say she was in the neighborhood and wondered if she could stop by for a visit. Albert had been head-over-heels in love with Hannah when they had been at university together but hadn't kept in touch over the years, so Albert was in mixed emotions about her. But curiosity got the better of him, and he invited her to stop by. She said she'd be by about threeish and got directions to the chalet. As it was almost noon, Albert decided to do it right and made a dash to town for a lavish meal and a few bottles of Bollinger's Grand Annee and had everything ready when Fraulein Mueller arrived.

When Hannah rang the front doorbell, Albert sprang to answer it. At the first look, the intervening 20 years melted away, and to Albert, it was as though they had been lovers and friends in grad school just yesterday.

"Please, won't you come in, Hannah," said Albert as he led her into the living room. "Let me look at you; you haven't changed a bit; you are just as lovely as I remember you from our school days!"

"You are too kind, Albert, but you always were," Hannah said. "It's quite a place you have here," she added.

"Yes, I got the most amazing deal when I bought the chalet; I bought it for delinquent taxes. The old owner left without a word and never came back. I got not only the house but three magnificent autos out in the garage too. Tell me, Hannah, how have you been, and what have you been up to? Oh, and can I get you something to drink, a glass of ice water or a glass of champagne?" Albert asked.

"As hot as it is, either would do; I'll leave it up to you, Albert," Hannah replied.

"Silly girl," thought Albert, "Champagne it is."

"Please make yourself comfortable and I'll be right back," Albert said as he made his way to the kitchen to retrieve one of the bottles of Bollinger's, two glasses, and a bucket full of ice.

When he returned, she asked to use the restroom, and he showed her the way. He then returned to the living room and popped the cork on the Bollinger's and poured them both a flute full.

When she returned and was seated, he proposed a toast to old times, and they both drank the flutes right down. Over the rest of the bottle, they talked about old times and brought each other up to date on their lives. He then took her on a tour of the house and then the grounds and the autos in the garage, and she seemed very impressed by it all. When he asked if she would stay for dinner, she replied she would stay as long as he liked!

This statement sent his mind reeling, as Hannah was always remembered as the one who got away, the girl he should have married. She was probably the reason that he never married, as no other woman could hold a candle to her. When he came back to reality, he found himself holding hands with her as they strolled along the property and decided they would have a picnic in the shade of the forest as they did when they were at school.

Of course, this time around, it wouldn't be just frankfurters and potato salad. This time he'd do it right, and he did.

They dined on a small salad, fine marbled steaks, white asparagus, and a Schwarzwälder Kirschtorte for dessert, a local favorite! They also managed to polish off another bottle of Bollinger's and then lay down upon the blanket side by side and talked again about old times.

A hundred meters away, their every movement was watched over by the dark fairies. They wondered what the arrival of the human female would mean to the King & Queen, and when Hannah and Albert got up and made their way back to the chalet, the fairies left and headed back for their meeting with the King and Queen and the rising of the solstice moon.

When Hannah and Albert got back to the chalet, Hannah excused herself to use the restroom, and Albert put away the remains of the picnic. The only thing he saved was the Schwarzwälder kirschtorte of which they had only eaten half. After disposing of the rest, Albert ran upstairs to use the master bedroom bathroom and then returned to the living room to await Hannah's arrival.

By this time, the sun had almost set, so he turned on two of the lamps but turned them all the way down low for a romantic setting and wondered how Hannah felt about that. He didn't have long to puzzle that as Hannah came out of the restroom in the nude and walked over to Albert, pulled him to her, and gave him a long, slow, wet kiss that seemed to last forever. When she let him go, she started to unbutton his shirt, and a few seconds later, he was as naked as she. He started out slow, making love to her with a lot of foreplay, the way he remembered she liked, and by the time they were through, Albert felt like he was 25 years old again!

They both walked to the restroom and got into the shower together, just like they used to and washed each other's bodies, and when they were through, they toweled one another dry.

They didn't get dressed, but Albert led her into the kitchen and grabbed another bottle of champagne, took out the Schwarzwälder Kirschtorte and cut it in half, which he gave to her as he grabbed a couple of flutes and the bottle and led her out to the front deck, where they set together on a couch cuddling as the full solstice moon rose over the trees turning the tree and shrubs in the front yard into a fairyland.

There were lightning bugs everywhere, or at least they thought they were. There were some lightning bugs, but there was something else glowing in the dark too. As the lovers watched, little naked people danced before their eyes. They were about 70 millimeters tall!

"Albert, what a magical place you have; I believe those are light fairies," said Hannah with joy.

"Had you asked me this afternoon if I believed in fairy magic, I would have laughed, but now I'm a believer! I always thought that light and dark fairies were old folklore! But look at them all, this ist Wunderbar, Wunderbar," he exclaimed!

They sat transfixed by the light fairies watching their flights and their games until the sun rose, and they all flew away.

When the fairies had left, they finally snapped out of the spell; only then realizing they had sat for some 7 hours, never saying a word nor touching the Schwarzwälder kirschtorte or the unopened champagne.

They were quiet for a moment until Albert said, "Let's have some breakfast as I'm starving; how about you, Hannah?"

"Yes, please, I could eat something," she replied.

As Albert cooked breakfast, neither said a word as they went over in their minds what they had seen. They even questioned whether it was all real, but they knew in their hearts that it was. When breakfast was prepared, they both broke into a conversation that lasted half an hour!

Over in the dark fairy compound, all the fairies assembled in the great house where the King and Queen sat reading the latest reports on Albert and Hannah. Then they questioned in detail all that had been watching the chalet before whispering amongst themselves before coming to their conclusion, announcing that upon the Autumnal Equinox, they would move on Albert and Hannah, too if she was still there, as the prison escapee they had killed on the Spring Equinox and placed in their ice cave would last the tribe until then.

Hannah spent the next two weeks at Albert's chalet before returning to her townhouse in Munich. On the night before she left, Albert went down on one knee and proposed to Hannah. She accepted, and they set a wedding date of September first, the date that Hannah's parents had married.

While Hannah headed home to Munich, Albert headed back to Strasbourg to tell the news to his business partner Hermann Richter and buy Hannah an engagement ring and a wedding band. To Hermann, he said he would be gone arranging the wedding and other things and probably wouldn't be back until late October at the earliest. In fact, Albert was thinking of selling out his half of the partnership and retiring to his chalet.

He was thinking of selling the 1939 Mercedes-Benz W31 type G4. As one of only 57 ever built, it should bring a pretty pfennig, and the Audi Q7 could go too as he needed the space for his and Hannah's car. He would keep the 1936 Auburn boat-tailed speedster 852 for himself and would also sell either his Mercedes or the Porsche. The Mercedes was nicer, but the Porsche was more practical. He would keep the chalet and probably sell his house in Strasbourg.

When Hannah's rings were ready, he drove to Munich to Hannah's townhouse and got down on his knee again and placed the engagement ring on the third finger of her left hand. He arose and gave her a kiss that she would never forget, and when he opened his eyes, tears were streaming down her face while she had the biggest smile that he had ever seen; they were tears of joy. She took his hand and took him to her bedroom, where they made love for at least an hour. In the afterglow, he told her of his plans for his house and automobiles and asked if she would live with him in the Black Forest. When she heard this, she started crying again and told him she would love to live there; of all the places on Earth, the chalet was her favorite, and so it was settled.

Albert stayed with Hannah in Munich for a fortnight as she settled her affairs and met with her parents; they heartily approved of Albert. Then it was off to Strasbourg to meet Albert's parents, who were overjoyed that Albert was finally getting married and to such a lovely girl. While they were there, Albert sold his house and his half-ownership of Higglemier and Richter at a good price. He sold his Mercedes-Maybach S 560 4Matic, the 1939 Mercedes-Benz W31 type G4, and the Audi Q7 for slightly more than $4,000,000 Euros. Albert's working days were over; perhaps he'd garden as a hobby, and Hannah would continue painting, not for the money but for the joy that it brought her. So, towards the end of July, they returned to the chalet and set up permanent housekeeping. They decided to have their reception at the chalet and were busy renting a floor of rooms at the local hotel; their parents would stay at the house along with Hannah's sister Anna and her husband. After the reception, Albert and Hannah would fly to Hawaii for two weeks on Maui before they returned and settled down.

They had missed the July full moon, but on the rising of the August full moon, they were once again sitting naked on their front deck with a bottle of champagne for themselves and an offering of a bowl of fresh fruit for their guests.

As the moon rose, there came the light fairies who once again did their magic dance. It wasn't too long before they noticed the bowl of fresh fruit, which they all flew around but didn't touch. Then, a male and female fairy flew over to Albert and Hannah and hovered and motioned to the bowl of fruit. Albert said, "Ja, meine Freunde, die alles für dich sind, helfen dir bitte!"

The pair bowed to Albert and Hannah, and Hannah and Albert bowed in return. In a high-pitched voice, the male fairy said something, and all the other fairies hovered over the bowl until the pair made their choices. When they had, the rest joined in the feast as Albert and Hannah made a toast to the fairies, saying, "Zum Wohl."

As before, the fairies flew all around them, sometimes holding hands and flying in a circle. Albert and Hannah, as before, sat amazed but this time holding hands. When the fairies eventually landed and then paired up and went making love, Albert and Hannah joined them, making love on the couch. When they came out of their love trance, all the fairies were flying around them and watching their every move. When they sat up, they heard what must have been a fairy cheer. What

Hannah didn't know at the time was that she was now pregnant.

As before, they sat and watched the fairies until the sun rose, but this time, before they flew away, they flew over to Albert and Hannah, and all bowed to them. Albert and Hannah returned the bow and said, "We wish you happiness and peace." And the fairies, as one, said the same thing back to them. This time, Albert and Hannah heard them distinctly.

Before long, September first came, and Albert and Hannah were married and hosted their reception at the chalet. A great time was had by all, including the light fairies who kept well hidden but enjoyed the festival as well as the humans. 100 meters away on the edge of the forest, the black fairies observed everything. In about three weeks' time, they would make their move on Albert and Hannah to secure enough food to last them not only through the winter but through the next Autumnal Equinox.

An hour or so during the reception, Albert and Hannah made their escape and headed for the Munich airport. They caught their airliner and awoke about an hour before they landed in Hawaii. They spent their first week flying here and there, seeing many things, but they spent their second week lying on the beach under the shade of palm trees, with a Mai Tai in their hands, watching the tide come in and go out for the perfect honeymoon!

They arrived back in Germany the week before the Autumnal Equinox to find their house was in pristine condition as their parents and friends had cleaned up the mess and had set their garbage out and even collected their mail and trimmed the lawns. They spent most of that week going between their parents' houses and shopping. On the day before the Autumnal Equinox, they returned to the chalet, and as the sun was setting, a delegation of dark fairies headed by their King and Queen approached Albert and Hannah and invited them to a feast tomorrow night at their village.

Unlike the light fairies, they were all dressed in business suits and long dresses, and their voices could be clearly heard. It was their harvest festival and since Albert and Hannah were their new neighbors, they thought it would be a friendly gesture to invite them to their feast.

Knowing only the light fairies, Albert and Hannah said they would be happy to attend, and it was agreed that an hour or so before sunset, they would return and guide them to their village. And so, it was set.

The very next day, Albert and Hannah were all excited about going to the fairies' feast. What a wonderful place they had here in the forest, and wearing their best formal attire, they eagerly awaited the coming of the dark fairies.

When the sun was on the low horizon, they saw the same fairy delegation emerge from the woods, so they walked up to meet them. When they entered the woods, they came upon a well-worn path, and they followed it a mile or so until they came to the dark fairy village. As they entered the village, all the fairies walking in front of them moved to the sides of the street just as a tree limb suspended by ropes came swinging down and struck them from behind, knocking them down, whereupon the fairies sprang on them with ropes and tied them down.

Soon, all the dark fairies were dancing around and around them, chanting some rhyme. This went on for several minutes until the King and Queen came out of the long house and made their speech to their subjects about how their food supply was guaranteed for another year. Then they called for the executioners to come forth and slay the humans.

That was the last thing the dark fairy King and Queen ever said as all the light fairies attacked and killed them both, as well as the executioners. While this was happening, both Albert and Hannah were set free from their bonds and were guided out of the forest while the dark fairy slaughter carried on. When they were through, there wasn't a single dark fairy alive. By the time the sun rose, the entire village and all the dead dark fairies had been thrown onto a funeral pyre and turned to ashes.

By the time the full moon rose, both Albert and Hannah had been to the doctors and were in perfect shape, except for Hannah, who found out she was pregnant. So, when the moon rose, and the light fairies came, they had a feast and celebration like no other. And on the summer solstice, Hannah gave birth to her son, Hans, and they all lived happily ever after!

MURDER AT THE MUSEUM

It was freezing outside. Jeffrey Cummings made his way across campus against a stiff northern breeze. He was going to be late if he didn't hurry. Too much studying and too little time. He had begun his job as a janitor at the University's Natural History Museum as a way of funding his senior year trip to Maui. Now 90 days away from picking up his masters, it had paid the bills and kept him afloat these last two years.

The Museum had closed an hour ago and the staff was probably already gone. Just Doctor Grey, the museum's head, would still be there awaiting Jeffrey's arrival. He trudged on into the teeth of a gale until he turned the corner in front of the dental college and the wind suddenly stopped, almost causing him to fall on the slippery sidewalk. Down the block and across the street, he could see the two black lion statues that guarded the front entrance to the museum.

Having to dodge a new electric "Lyric" as he crossed the street brought him out of his "I'm late to work" trance and back to reality. As he walked up the sidewalk between the lions, he could see Doctor Grey standing by the door, looking a bit impatient.

"Good evening, Doctor Grey; sorry I'm running a little late."

"Listen, Jeffrey, our present from the JPL and NASA is up and running. I've just finished opening the display but I'm afraid I've left you a bit of a mess."

"I'll get right on it, Doctor Grey, first thing."

"Goodnight, Jeffrey," Doctor Grey mumbled as he hurried from the building.

The present that Doctor Grey had mentioned was a rather large meteorite that had been found in the Antarctic several years ago, that an alumnus had steered toward Doctor Grey. Since its arrival, the good Doctor has been all a-twitter for the last five months about this prized specimen. Jeff made his way to the meteor exhibit overlooking the University's excellent Dinosaur collection. A large packing case overflowing with foam peanuts and bubble wrap greeted his eyes. Fifteen minutes later, the exhibit hall had been returned to its former pristine condition, and Jeffrey took the time to study the Museum's newest exhibit. To the layman, a chunk of space debris, burned black by its fiery entry into Earth's atmosphere. To the Doctor, another fascinating piece of the great puzzle of life. To Jeffrey, just another thing to dust. With the cleanup complete, he went down to his closet to get a floor buffer and wax to start his regular duties.

He mopped and buffed the big front lobby, ramps, and staircases, and when he turned the machine off, he thought he heard a faint clicking noise but put it down to the high winds. He turned on the lights in the main exhibition hall and began buffing the marble floor to a bright shine. For the next two hours, he cleaned the great hall, and as he finished, he suddenly had a strange feeling come over him that something was missing? He couldn't quite place what it was, but after two years, he knew the floor plan like the back of his hand, and something had changed. As he turned off the machine, he heard it distinctly. A sound like someone walking with taps on their shoes on the hard marble floor. But it stopped almost as soon as he heard it.

Someone was in the building. The alarms hadn't gone off so they had to be hiding here since closing. Very casually, Jeffrey started to the office to call the campus police. Out of the main hall, down a long dark corridor to the behind-the-scenes area of the Museum. Halfway down the darkened hallway, he heard the clicking sound again. This time, though, it was a lot faster and it was getting louder. Jeffrey lost all pretenses as he ran to the office and began struggling with his great keychain. Under normal circumstances, he could have opened the door in seconds, but his hands were shaking.

As he found the key, something hit him hard from behind and sent him crashing through the office door. Fortunately, he hit his head on the marble floor and knocked himself unconscious. This was very lucky because Jeffrey never felt himself being torn in two.

"Let's go over your story, Doctor Grey, one more

time," said Lt. Osbourne of the campus police force as he checked his sergeant's notebook. "Says here that you say the Cummings boy was a little late coming to work tonight. Is he often late, Doc?"

"Jeffrey was a good employee, a good student, and a good friend. He was seldom ever late, Lt."

The Lt. continued to scan the notebook as he said, "Did he mention why he was running late tonight?"

"No, as I told the sergeant and before him the patrol-man, I asked Jeffrey to see to the mess on the second floor and then left him to his duties. We hardly spoke at all."

At this point, their conversation was interrupted by the sergeant who announced that they had finished the search, and the building was secure and empty. Now they were awaiting the arrival of the State Police and their tracking dog.

When Jeffrey had been driven through the office door, he had set off a burglar alarm. A police cruiser was barely a block away and was at the museum in no time at all. He parked so he could see three sides of the building and waited for backup to arrive. When two other cars came, the officers checked all the doors and windows on the ground floor and found them all to be locked. The sergeant had then sent Officer Patterson to retrieve the Doctor and had him open the doors. By this time, the entire campus security force had arrived, and they began a systematic search of the building and the surrounding area. It wasn't very long before they came across Jeffrey's remains, half of which had been dragged several yards down the hallway from the office. Since then, Doctor Grey had been both an instructor and a star witness to the sergeant and now the lieutenant. The medical examiner had just finished his examination of the body when the lieutenant arrived.

Lieutenant John Osbourne had been a policeman since his enlistment in the army during the Vietnam War. In the 50 years since, he had been a big city Homicide Detective, eventually rising to precinct Captain. He had retired after 30 years as a deputy chief and had sought to spend his time hunting, fishing, and playing cards with the boys. After a couple of years of that, he found himself bored to death and desperately wanting to go back to work. Besides, 59 was hardly the age to retire. Four years ago, he became the second in command for the University's Security Forces behind the captain, who was due for retirement himself at the end of this semester. Lt. Osbourne had already been given the nod as his replacement.

This was good and bad. It meant another large raise, but it also meant turning the running of the day-to-day affairs of the department to the sergeant, soon to be Lieutenant Brown. This might be his last real case as nothing like this had ever happened on campus, and probably never would again. The detective inside him was dying to get out and run amok. Something was rotten in the state of Denmark. Something was way out of line here. It wasn't only the state of the body. He had seen worse in the Nam and almost as bad in the city. But since crime knows no boundaries, he wasn't surprised that it had happened here.

No, it wasn't the state of the body, but something was

amiss. Jeffrey had been torn in two by something or someone. John's dealings with Colombian gangs had introduced him to the effects a chainsaw could have on the human body. And a chainsaw was obviously the murder weapon here, although they hadn't found it. Nor could anyone give a reason why anyone would do such a thing. In the 206 years of the university's existence, there had only been two murders, both of which were quickly solved. John knew that this one wouldn't be that easy, but solve it he would; he had no doubt about that. By now, the sergeant had interviewed all the employees and was correlating his notes. The employees were doing a painstaking search to see if any of their exhibits were missing, but so far, everything seemed intact. John knew that if he could find the reasons behind the murder, he could solve it.

John had worked that morning and afternoon, and around 6 p.m., he got the call he had been waiting for from the Medical Examiner's office. The autopsy results were in, and they were as strange as the case had become. The ME said that Jeffrey had been bitten in two, and not by anything the ME or any of his assistants had ever seen. They had submitted their findings, as well as the body, to the State Police Crime Lab to see if they could shed any light on the mystery. Jokingly, John had asked if maybe one of the dinosaurs had done it and was surprised to hear the ME say perhaps they did. They both had a laugh before hanging up.

At eight o'clock, the lieutenant called off the search and interviews and sent his investigators home as he went back to the station to write up his reports for the captain and, more importantly, the board of regents. As he left the museum, he was approached by two local reporters whom he brushed off with a "no comment" as he swept past them on his way to his cruiser.

Doctor Grey sent his staff home, except for his secretary Janet, whom he asked to stay after and help him search for anything missing. She agreed to stay and help but since she hadn't eaten all day, she begged off to go get a burger or something. Doctor Grey realized he hadn't eaten since yesterday and told her to keep looking, and he would go to Morey's and get them both a good meal instead. Morey's, one of the classier restaurants on campus, brought a big smile to Janet's face, and she readily agreed. Grabbing his hat and coat, the Doctor went out the door, locking it behind him.

Janet Whitelaw was a grad student, like Jeffrey, working on her MBA and serving as Doctor Grey's "Girl Friday." She played a crucial role in managing the day-to-day operations of the museum, allowing the doctor to focus on his research. In return, the doctor made sure to keep her satisfied and happy. Janet was not only an administrative whiz but also incredibly attractive. She possessed an irresistible combination of a stunning figure, long blonde hair, bright blue eyes, and a sky-high IQ of over 200, despite being only 23 years old. She had a strong influence over the doctor and many others, although she rarely abused that power.

At that moment, Janet was on the fourth floor of the museum, meticulously going through the gemstone collection, cross-referencing the items in her catalog with those on display. Jeffrey's death had greatly shaken her, but she tried to stay focused on her work to distract herself from the gruesome murder. As she was halfway through her catalog, she heard a peculiar scratching sound coming from below. She froze in place, her blood running cold, before realizing that it was probably the doctor returning with her dinner. Setting her work aside, she left the room and walked down the hall to get a view of the staircases and ramps that led up to the fourth floor.

To her relief, there was nothing out of the ordinary. She attributed the noise to her frazzled nerves and dismissed it. Just as she was about to turn back, she heard a distinct clicking sound from below, as if someone was walking with a rhythmic tapping of their shoes. Janet turned and gazed down the staircases, catching a glimpse of a shadow on the second floor from her peripheral vision. A jolt of fear surged through her body, causing her hair to stand on end. She knew what she had seen, but she refused to accept it. She stared fixedly at the second-floor landing, hoping to catch another glimpse of the shadow and prove to herself that she wasn't going insane. She prayed not to see it again because if her vision were accurate, she was in grave danger just like Jeffrey. There was no way to escape except down those steps; there was no way to call for help from the fourth floor. The only phone available above the second-floor offices was in the fifth-floor planetarium. Janet would appear foolish if she called 911 over a hallucination, but the image of Jeffrey's mutilated body haunted her thoughts. Although his face and upper torso were covered up, she couldn't forget his dismembered legs and intestines strewn down the hallway. The fact that the perpetrator was still at large and the lower part of Jeffrey's legs was missing added to her terror. Janet berated herself for agreeing to work alone in such circumstances. Foolish or not, she had no choice but to call the police.

Silently and cautiously, Janet ascended the steps toward the fifth floor. When she reached the landing between floors, she peered over the edge. There was nothing below. She continued her ascent, pausing halfway up to realize that she had been holding her breath. She took several deep breaths before rushing up the remaining steps to the fifth floor. Her initial panic began to subside as she noticed an open door to the planetarium. However, to be certain of her safety, she glanced over the railing and locked eyes with death, who stared back at her from the second floor.

Overwhelmed by terror, Janet let out a piercing scream and sprinted in blind panic through the plane-tarium doors, desperately making her way to the office and the telephone. To her dismay, the office door was locked. In the distance, she could hear death approaching as it passed by the third floor. Frantically looking for a solution, she seized the velvet rope holder, hurled it through the office window, and crawled through the shattered glass and across the floor, finally reaching the phone just as death reached the fourth floor and turned toward the fifth. In a state of desperation, she dialed for an outside line and then dialed 911, fully aware that death had entered her office.

"Hello, 911 operator, ; how can I help you? Hello, 911

operator; how can I help you. ? Hey, Marty, I got a 911 call from the planetarium, but nobody responds. Should I send someone out there?"

"Which one, Stella?"

"Let's see.... it's the one at the Natural Science Museum, Marty."

"Ah, Stella, isn't that the one where that student was found cut in two?"

"Oh my god......911 dispatch to campus police; we have problems at the Natural Science Museum, dispatch an officer immediately over..."

"Officer on the way 911 dispatch...."

Lieutenant Osbourne was just sitting down to have dinner with his son and his son's fiancée and the Reverend Vaughn who had just agreed to marry them this June when the happy couple graduated. They'd just drunk a second toast to the good Rev. when John's cell phone went off. He tried not to jump when it did. John excused himself and took the phone into the den. It was Sergeant Brown who had called him.

"Lieutenant, I'm sorry to bother you at home, but we've had another murder at the museum. It was Doctor Grey's secretary Janet Whitelaw this time, and it's worse than the first one."

"I'm on my way Sergeant, ETA in ten minutes."

"There's no hurry, Lieutenant. We got the killer this time!"

"Well, who is it, man?"

"It's Doctor Grey, sir. Found him covered in her blood."

"Don't move a muscle, sergeant. I'm on my way. Keep

the doctor there, I wish to question him. Have you called the lab?"

"Yes, sir, the State Police crime Crime Lab is on the way."

"Has the Doctor confessed, sergeant?"

"I think the doctor is trying for an insanity defense sir. He claims to have seen two juvenile allosauruses' kill Ms. Whitelaw. He keeps repeating they're alive, they're alive."

"I'm on my way, sergeant, ; keep the students out of there and for God's sake, don't let the press get a hold of this until we can get a handle on things."

He hung up the phone and returned to the dining room to explain as little as possible to his guests. Yes there had been another murder at the museum, but apparently, they had a suspect in custody. He told them not to wait as he would be late and left them to their meal. He retrieved his service revolver and took a double double-shot swig of some Kentucky Bourbon, grabbed his coat and hat and headed across campus to the museum.

When he arrived, he was met near the entrance with half a dozen microphones were shoved in the direction of his face and asked half a dozen voices for a comment. He declined and made his way between the uniformed officers at the door, where he was joined by Sergeant Brown.

"This way, sir, I've got him parked in the office on the second floor. Mind the blood stains, sir."

The white and black marble floor was awash in a crimson swath as if something bleeding very badly had been dragged down the stairs and across the lobby towards a basement door. There, by the door, a body lay covered by an ME's blanket.

"Just a minute, sergeant; I want to view the body."

"Ah, no, you don't, sir. It's worse than the boy. She was about four months pregnant, and he cut out the baby!"

The sergeant was correct. When Lt. Osbourne turned back the blanket, what he saw forced his bile towards his throat. The first thing he noticed was the nose was missing, and so were the ears. As he pulled the blanket further back, he barely noticed her exposed breasts, for his eyes were pulled toward the gaping hole in her stomach! As if to answer an unasked question, the sergeant pulled a plastic bag from his coat, at the bottom of which lay a tiny little hand! John covered up the remains, not even looking at her legs that were torn here and there all the way to her ankles.

Instead, he stood and made for the door to gain some fresh air but pulled up short, remembering the reporters outside and silently cursed the gods under his breath. The girl had sent his mind spinning back to the Nam, where he remembered the village that had joined the US inoculation program.

He had been escorting a group of doctors and corpsmen back to a village that they had previously visited. What they found there still haunted him after all these years. Instead of the 112 people they had inoculated, they found a pile of 112 arms. The Viet Cong had left a message, and the people of surrounding villages got the message. A message that was not lost on the medical personnel or a 19-year-old MP. At that moment, John knew that we had lost the war and he lost any plans for reenlistment.

"You going to be okay, Lieutenant?"

John snapped out of it. "Yeah, I'll be fine; just give me a minute to catch my breath. Let's talk to the Doctor," John said, shaking off the old memories.

As they climbed the stairs; to avoid the blood on the ramp, John noticed two bloody footprints descending the ramp from the third floor. "Doctor Grey's footprints, Sergeant Brown?"

"Yes, sir, they match exactly the shoes he was wearing, they have already been removed from him and sent with the rest of the evidence to the State Police Crime Lab, sir."

"Very good, Charlie. You know the regents have told me the new pecking order is here after the captain retires. My recommendation for you to replace me has been approved by the board, and you should be getting the official word very soon."

"Why, thank you, sir, for your kind words. I won't let you down, sir. He's in here, sir; mind the blood, sir. That's where the attack began in the other office.'

As Lt. Osbourne entered the second office, he saw a man sitting in the middle of the room, staring off into space. He bore no resemblance to the mild manner, immaculately dressed, middle-aged doctor of natural history that John had met on several occasions. Gone was any pretense of humanity and any sign of intelligence. The man was obviously mad, quite insane by any standard. He had seen too many similar faces in the Nam that he could never forget.

"I want this man taken to the hospital immediately for observation," John said to the sergeant as he rolled his eyes and looked toward the ceiling.

"Yes sir, I'll get the 'medics' here at once," said the sergeant as he grabbed the phone.

Doctor Grey never said a thing that day or ever again and until the day that he died, which was barely a month later. After learning that the prosecutor wouldn't charge him with the murders; as everyone thought him insane, he seemed to lose the will to live. An airborne virus attacked the doctors weakened system, and he was dead from a viral infection in a week's time. The murder investigations were officially closed, and life returned back to normal on campus.

The semester ended, and John's son and now daughter-in-law graduated and were married on campus and were soon off on their honeymoon. The Chief retired amid much pomp and circumstance, and for the second time in his life, John was promoted to Captain. He had almost forgotten about the questions he had about the murders. What with the murders stopping after Janet's and the removal of the Doctor, life in the last four months had returned to its small town charm. The only problems were generally drinking related, but hey, it was a college town. It was a rather bad shock to hear the request for a policeman at the Natural History Museum. Something made him turn his car around and tell the dispatcher that he would take the call.

It all came back to him like the adrenaline rush of a punch in the nose. His mind focused on all the doubts he had to the doctor's complicity in the murders. As he entered the building, he was met by the new museum head.

Doctor Marcus Tiberius Hoover took John's hand in a hearty handshake and welcomed him into the museum. "I'm surprised you came so quickly, Captain, to our little loss. A patrolman could have taken care of this. You needed have come for the theft of two eggs. Please come with me, and I'll show you what we found."

John followed the doctor up the stairs to the second floor Dino exhibit. Down the rows, past fossilized statues of creatures beginning with a Woolly Mammoth and Saber Toothed Tiger, barely 20,000 years old, backward in time past various and sundry monsters from little Utah Raptor, past the Allosaurus, beyond the giant duck bill and the head from the T-Rex, to where there was a dinosaur nest exhibit. Doctor Hoover stopped and knelt down to a nest and pointed to where two eggs were missing.

"According to our records, there were two more eggs in this nest. When I took over here, we did a complete inventory, and this was the only thing missing. We called our insurance, and they said to have someone make the police report. Captain, do you think this has anything to do with my unfortunate predecessor?"

"That's hard to say, Doctor Hoover. Tell me, what would these eggs be worth on the 'Black Market'?"

"To a private collector? Prime eggs from Ornitholestes, that's hard to say, Captain. Upwards of six figures, I'd guess. Oh, here is a copy of the photo showing the nest's configuration when it was assembled."

"What's this blue stuff where the eggs were, Doctor? It's not in the photograph. It looks like some sort of acid?"

"We don't know as yet, Captain. We sent a sample over to the labs to have it analyzed. Hasn't come back yet? My Grad student Mary thought someone might have poured it over the eggs and somehow loosened them from the rest?"

When he heard the word poured, something caused John to look up above the nest site to the balcony above. The same blue shiny substance was glinting in the overhead lights on the edge of the balcony. "What's directly above us, Doctor?"

"Directly above is our gem and mineral displays. Various displays from petrified wood to meteorites, Captain, but why?"

"Let's take a walk up there, shall we, doctor? I have a hunch about this."

"As you like, Captain. Let me turn the lights on up there. Wouldn't do to fall over that balcony! Ah, that's better, now follow me."

As he walked down the hall, John could already see what he was looking for. Sitting beside the end of the wall by where a balcony overlooked the displays below sat a large blackish object. From the bottom of this rock was a telltale blue stain that ran downhill from the meteor over the edge of the balcony. When he peered over the edge, he found himself staring at a clutch of dinosaur eggs. "Perhaps, doctor, we may find that your eggs weren't stolen but were dissolved... or hatched...."

"No, that would be impossible, Captain. Ornitholestes, or as you call him, Allosaurus, has been extinct for over 130 million years. It could hardly have hatched because..."

That was as far as the doctor got before the creature had grabbed him, pulled him up to its mouth, and bit him in two, and the doctor was gone. It shoved the rest of the doctor into its maw, threw its head back again, and swallowed the rest. It then turned to Captain Osbourne, who was lining the creature up in the sight of his Mac 10, and lowered its head for a bite.

When Mary, Doctor Hoover's 'Girl Friday,' reported for work the next morning, she knew something was wrong but couldn't put a finger on it until she went to see why the lights were on on the third floor. She found that the new meteor had been knocked over, which seemed impossible as it weighed about 700 lbs. There seemed to be a pool of blue liquid foaming around on the balcony. When she looked into a display room, she found all that was left of Captain John Michael Osbourne. His right arm and hand, still holding a now empty Mac 10. The VC would have loved the irony.

The two Allosaurus had grown in the steam tunnels that crisscrossed the campus. Something in that meteor had tripled their growth rate. First, rats and pets became their prey, then bums and junkies, until they returned to the museum. That night, the pair hopped aboard a stopped freight train loaded with Angus cattle and bound for Florida. By the time the cars were cut to the siding outside Miami, all of the cattle were gone, and the Allosaurs, now accompanied by a hungry brood of 12 hatchlings, headed out into the Everglades and that warm Florida sun.

The murders were never solved, and in the coming years, the campus gained a certain reputation, ala Jack the Ripper, and was the subject of much talk and an increase in wealth for many local businessmen.

John's arm was given to the museum by his family and now resides in the justly famous "taxidermical section" of the Museum of Natural History, still clutching the Mac 10.

HANSEL AND GRETEL
REVISITED

Ja, it's nice to meet you too, Jakob and Wilhelm. So, you ist the Brothers Grimm, eh? Ja, I heard of you, and you have come for mein story? Das ist gut, das ist sehr gut! Come sitzen und I'll tell you. Ve haft to be quick because they almost have the scaffold done. Well, where to begin?

Ja, it all started when Papa married that Eva woman. She was the village whore, but poor Papa didn't know. As soon as she came into our lives, everything started going wrong for me and mien sister Gretel. And, I want to make one thing clear no matter what it says in de papers; there was never any monkey business between us but ve were da best of friends.

Papa's business of gathering sticks into a bundle, then taking them to town and selling them was thriving when the stepmother came to live in our little forest house. She was never satisfied with anything or anybody. She was such a shicser, oy! But Papa liked her, and because we loved Papa we went along. For such a little woman, she could eat like two grown men. I've never seen anyone eat like that. And you know how everybody has four canine teeth? She had eight!

Everything was still going okay until the bottom dropped out of the 'bundle of sticks' market. Suddenly Papa couldn't sell a bundle of sticks because of something called "coal?" It wasn't long before our larder was nearing empty. Gretel and I barely had a crust of bread to eat, but Step-mama seemed to be getting fatter. We noticed all the little bunnies, birdies, and squirrels around our house suddenly disappeared. It wasn't long, however, when Gretel and I were awakened one night by Step-mama and Papa arguing. Papa was saying no, he wouldn't do it and to drop the subject, and Step-mama was telling Papa that if he didn't do what she told him, then he wouldn't get any more visits from Miss Pussy Cat. Gretel and I didn't know what to make out of it, but Papa seemed to change his mind then and said he'd think about it.

Early the next morning, after Papa went off to cut some sticks, Step-mama took us deep into the woods where we had never been before. She said we were to build a big fire to keep warm, and she and Papa would be back in a little while to take us home. Well, we built a big fire and ate the piece of bread she had given us and went to sleep, and when we woke up, it was almost dark when we heard Papa calling us. He soon found us and, for some reason, seemed really happy to see us and carried us home on his broad shoulders, kissing and hugging us all the while.

When we got home, Step-mama didn't seem all that happy. Step-mama must have walked into a tree because she had a big bruise under her eye and was very quiet.

Everything was soon back to normal, as there seemed to be a new market "overseas" for bundles of sticks. As winter turned to spring and spring to summer, everything seemed okay until one night, near the solstice. Step-mama got us up early one morning before dawn after Papa had gone to the string makers to get another roll of string to tie up his bundles with. Step-mama said we were to go and help Papa gather some sticks, so off we went in a direction that we had never gone before because it led deep into the woods where the bears and wolves live. After many hours of walking, we came to a place where Step-mama said we would be very near Papa, and he would come for us after our work was done. She gave us a loaf of purple rye bread to eat for lunch and left us to our chores.

We went right to work and kept at it, so by noon, we had 30 bunches of sticks ready to be bundled by Papa. We took a break down by the creek, and with fresh cold water, we ate the loaf of rye bread between us. We rested a while, but when we got up to go back to work, both Gretel and I saw the strangest thing. All the sticks we had bundled began to get up and dance around and around. Seeing this, poor Gretel threw her dress over her eyes and went running and screaming through the woods. I, of course, followed after her. She hadn't run but a mile or so, still screaming at the top of her lungs until she ran headfirst into a tree and knocked herself out. By the time I found her, the sun was going down, and I decided to build a little fire and wait till Papa found us. But Papa didn't come, and we spent the night shivering in the forest. We slept till after the sun had risen high in the sky, then woke up hungry and sore all over. As we had eaten all the bread yesterday, there was nothing to eat, and we looked all around for berries and roots but couldn't find any. We walked along calling for Papa and finally found a little stream to drink from about dark. By the time the sun had risen the next day, we were as hungry as can be. We got up and drank as much as we could from the stream and began to walk along looking for Papa. It was about noon when we came upon the mushrooms.

Gretel was the first to see them, and even though I warned her they might be poisonous, she quickly picked and ate a handful and said that they were delicious. I soon, too, was picking and eating them. I ate a tummy full and, in the warmth of the sun, lay down and rested. Before too long, I heard a whispering sound. Gretel heard it too, and it said that we children should come this way if we wanted a candy treat. And who doesn't like ze candy Herr Grimms? Well, I can tell you that we ran through the woods, and there in a clearing was a house dat was made from gingerbread with icing and sugar-spun windows. Even though we had filled our bellies on the mushrooms, we dug right into the house, but soon a little ole lady came out and said we shouldn't eat her house and we should come inside before the bears ate us und, so we did.

But as soon as we did, she seemed to change, and her nose got long, and a mole appeared with two little hairs growing out of it on her chin, and her teeth got all pointy like Step-mamas. She said she would feed us, but Gretel, who had thrown her dress over her head again, said that the old lady was a witch and was going to eat us. The witch then proceeded to pretend to get a chicken ready to put in her oven, and when she bent over to see if it was hot enough, Gretel pushed her in and shut the oven door. While the old witch screamed and screamed, we ran and ran, and the very next day, we were awakened by Papa calling for us. We were soon in his big strong arms, and he was hugging and kissing us all the way home.

We were very dirty so while we took a bath Papa went into the kitchen and cooked and cooked a big roast. When we came down to eat, we noticed Step-mama wasn't there, and when we asked Papa about it, he just smiled and said she wouldn't be around anymore and to dig in. So, we did. I must say I never tasted anything quite as good as that roast. Papa said it was from an old recipe and it was only for special occasions. It was only at the trial that I was told her body was found hanging in the icehouse. All of it except the leg that we had for dinner that night. I had gone out to the privy when the angry mob came for us.

They came not to kill Step-mama but because they had found the bishop's mother in her little cottage, baking in the oven. I hid in the woods while they killed poor Gretel and Papa.

They had traced her death back to us because Gretel

had left her babushka there with the nametag sewn into the lining. The bishop was not amused and sent the roaring mob out to take revenge. I was picked up the next day and brought to town and trial. That was a quick five minutes, and then they said guilty, and I was to meet ze, hangman, as soon as a scaffold could be built. Ach, dis ist been one hell of a week for an eight-year-old boy.

I can see through this window that a large angry crowd has gathered; the carpenters are just finishing the crossbar and are testing the rope. I hope you guys will at least spell my name right. That's Hansel with one L. Well, I see the hangman is walking this way, so danke Herr Grimms for listening to mein tale of woe.

THE DARK

H e stood on the rim and looked out at the world, and the world was desert! As far as the eye could see, an unbroken plain of salt and sand stretched away to the horizon and beyond. The desert was colored brown and white, and yellow. A few cactus-looking plants hugged the rim wall, beyond which nothing grew. The heat: even here at the edge of the desert, was stifling. Wave upon wave of heat shimmered from the sand and played tricks on the eyes. Below, a dust devil spun and made lazy circles off to his right. It was the only sign of movement, the only sign of life. An odor of sulfur and salt tore at his nostrils while he considered his fate.

There could be no turning back; to do so meant a sure and painful death. Even now, he could hear the howls of the tracking beasts as they made their way across the valley behind him. An hour behind, maybe two, but as sure as the sun; that never set in the sky, they would soon be upon him. His mind raced to find an exit, some way out, but there was none. To die in the desert, or to be torn apart for the amusement of the Emperor and the Imperial Court, was his only choice. At least the desert was clean!

He checked his supplies, two maybe three days' rations of food, a week's worth of water, and one full and one-half empty charge for the laser rifle. And the one reason he kept running from them, the reason he was still alive, the reason he would never give up, the last remaining clutch of Dragon eggs. He closed up his pack, took a deep breath, and began running down the hill and into the desert.

When he reached the bottom of the hill, he turned left, away from the storm, and took a heading on the twin peaks of the Dragon Horns mountains, some 50 miles away. From above, the desert had looked flat, but after an hour or so, he came upon a gully; an ancient river, and ran into its cooling shade. Tired and out of breath, he rested in the cool and, taking off his pack, inspected its precious cargo.

Nestled in his spare shirt were twelve gems, all a different color. Hard as diamonds yet glowing from deep inside. The last clutch from the last of the great Wyrms. Now no bigger than ostrich eggs, yet when fully grown, they would sport an 80 ft wing span and weigh in at 5 tons. A dragon could fly for many weeks at 300 mph without stopping to land. Teeth that could crunch and eat a flyer and claws that could rip open a tank. Scales as hard as diamonds and their hot breath could melt any known metal. Not really fire, but a combination of several highly corrosive acids spit from an orifice under the dragon's tongue. But what made them really dangerous was their intelligence.

He closed the pack, took out his water jug, and took a long deep draw. He was bone tired and hadn't slept in many cycles. He had run about 150 miles since his flyer had been hit in his mad dash to escape. He knew he would have to sleep soon, but to stop would mean his death. He took another sip of the precious liquid, and as he did, he saw a reflection of light on top of the rim from where he had come. He shaded his eyes from the blinding sun and looked again. He could see them in their colorful uniforms, pretty colors, he thought. Made for parading, not for hunting. At least he would know where they were. He also saw the dust devil spinning at the base of the hill. That just might confuse the beasts for a while, he thought, as he capped the water jug and pulled himself up onto his tired feet.

He could no longer run but tried to trot down the gully and away from the rim. He tried to stay in the shadows to conserve what little energy he had left. It was hopeless, but still, he moved on. The trot soon became a walk, and after another hour, he was forced to rest.

He lay in the cool of a shadow and thought to take a brief rest but soon fell asleep and dreamed of his home planet and its rolling blue oceans.

He returned to his mother's cottage deep in a cool dark valley. He saw his brothers and sisters working the fields or picking grapes in the arbors. His mother was sitting and rocking his youngest sister under the big shade tree in the yard. He looked for his father but then remembered he was killed off the planet in the Dragon Wars. He was just back from killing the nest of the dragon that had eaten his father. A mating pair and a dozen nestlings. It had been a long campaign on two worlds. His unit alone killed a quarter million. He was drunk on blood and slaughter but very tired and listless. It was good to be back at home in the shade of the arbor. He could hear his mother calling to him, and then his brothers and sisters were calling too.

He awoke with a start and realized they were very near and closing in on him. That dream was from a long time ago when he was young and a dragon slayer. He had stolen the last clutch and run here from his old comrades, for he saw a way to make some easy money and buy himself some time. Instead, when he had the eggs in his possession, something began to change in him, not at first but soon and more and more each day. He was beginning to feel a strange kinship with them. He couldn't put a finger on it, but he knew he couldn't destroy or sell them. He must save them at all costs. They were the last of a once proud and mighty race, all but destroyed by his kind.

He peeked up over the rim of the gully and saw them a quarter mile away in two groups. One group tracked from behind, and another group to the one side, trying to get in front of him. He was up in an instant and running along the gully away from his pursuers. Two men and three tracking beasts were off on his left. After a few minutes, he gradually pulled ahead of the flankers.

Had he been able to see his backpack, he would have

noticed a multi-hued glow, and suddenly, his thoughts turned to lay an ambush for the flankers while he still had time. Something told him that a good spot was just ahead. He had never been to this planet before. Hadn't even known its name, Parlesia, or that everybody knew who he was and what he had done, or the rather large reward that the eggs and his head would bring. He was just beginning to realize that none of those compelling thoughts were his. To steal the eggs or to come to this planet. But when he held the eggs in his hands and felt the vibrations beat in time to the glow, nothing mattered. The eggs were love. He could no longer imagine killing them or that all-consuming hate after the death of his father.

As the gully made a large S curve, he saw that he had cut across the path of his flankers, and at the end of that curve, he saw the place that he had seen before in his mind. A small outcropping of rock pushed its way up from the desert floor. He raced to its base and began to climb up until he reached its top. He pulled his rifle off his back and took aim at his followers.

He dropped the two humans in quick succession and then turned his attention to the beasts. Off-world creatures that looked like a cross between the body of a bull with the head of a crocodile. As he fired on the humans, the beasts made a beeline for his perch. He shot the first two as they came, but then his weapon was empty. As he dropped his last clip of energy into the rifle, bright flashes of energy began streaking past his head, and a smell of ozone permeated the air. Although still a quarter mile away, the other group had found him and was running in his direction. A voice in his head told him to jump down and make a run for it.

He leaped from his perch and had begun to run when he heard the third beast growl close behind him. In the confusion of battle, he had forgotten that there were three. A fact that might soon cost him everything. Something nudged him and sent him sprawling to the ground. The massive tracking beast stood snarling above him; then, as it began to lower its head down to devour him, it was suddenly jerked up and backward. As it turned its head to snap at what was holding it, he saw the flea.

A sand crab held the tracking beast in its pincers. "Sand Crabs" or "Dragon Fleas" were mean, nasty little monsters that generally lived in or near dragon caves. He hadn't the time to wonder what this one was doing in the Great Polar Desert as the crab bit the struggling tracking beast in two and turned in his direction. He jumped to his feet as the ground began to tilt. Try as he might, he couldn't stop from sliding. He quit trying when a voice told him that he had to hurry, that this was the only way out. With a serene look of peace in his eyes and a silly-looking grin on his face, he began sliding down towards the crab's lair and into the dark.

The Sand Crabs trap was a simple hinged incline that would send a victim into the loving jaws of the Sand Crabs mate, but when he got to the bottom of the ramp, the waiting Sand Crab just looked him over but made no move to attack. He would have tried to run back up the ramp, but the trap had already reset itself, so, like it or not, he was in the Sand Crabs' lair with no hope of escape.

Gradually his eyes adjusted to the darkness as several shafts of light came through several holes in the rock up above, and he found himself surrounded not only by the Sand Crab but also the Sand Crabs victims. Piles of bones were neatly stacked against the walls of the cave as if in storage, and in the center, there were small piles of bone fragments. He slowly moved away from the Sand Crab when the trap door opened, and the other Sand Crab came in carrying half of the tracking beast in one of its claws. It dropped the body at the other Sand Crabs' feet, which cut the tracking beast in two, pushing one half to its mate and began to devour the other half.

While the Sand Crab was dining, he slowly backed away from the beasts searching for a way out of this predicament; he could vaguely see two tunnels leading from the lair when a Sand Crab came up from behind him and pushed him again and again towards the left tunnel. After a couple of shoves, he thought he understood the Sand Crab and started walking toward the tunnel when a blinding light from the trap door brought two of his pursuers into the Sand Crab's lair. They tried to regain their balance and aim their blasters at the crabs but were far too slow as the beasts grabbed them and cut them in two.

Why the beasts had let him go and perhaps showed him the way while immediately killing his enemies made no sense, but who was he to look for a gift Sand Crab in the mouth? He began to move down the darkening tunnel as quickly as he could! In a short while, he had to feel his way along the tunnel as the light was all but gone. A hundred yards later and he thought he saw the light ahead and continued toward it. It wasn't light as such, but a glowing fungus of some sort lined the tunnel on both sides and the ceiling. He continued on for several miles but had to stop and rest. He took a swig of water from the jug and poured a little into his hands to wash his face and eyes with but try as he might stay awake, he was soon lost in a deep sleep that lasted a full day. Again, he dreamt of his family farm and the rolling oceans of his home planet.

He awoke and couldn't remember for a while where he was and how he had got there; then, the glowing eggs in his pack brought him back to reality. Even with the pack closed, the eggs produce much more light than the glowing fungus. While his eyes focused, he opened the pack and sought out his meager food supplies. If he cut the food rations in half, they would give him four days' worth of energy; after that, in the shape he was in, he wouldn't last long. Since he had about three days' worth of water and a couple of energy packs that dissolved in water, he filled his cup and put one packet into it, and waited for it to dissolve. While he waited, he unwrapped the eggs and was almost blinded by their light. In the daylight, they would be just seen to glow a bit, but here in the darkness, they had shown like beacons. The twelve eggs each glowed a different color and pulsed in unison. They were beautiful beyond words, and somehow, he felt they emitted the feeling of love with every pulse.

His cup of water turned a light blue and was now piping hot and ready to drink. As he did, his mind raced to find a way out of there and what he would do with the eggs if he never found a way out. He couldn't go back into the sand crabs lair; he wasn't sure with what remained of his rifle's charge if he even had the energy to kill them both. As heavily armored as the crabs were, he rather doubted that his weapon would do little more than madden the crabs. No, better to keep going down this tunnel as occasionally there was a crack high above that let light in the darkness. When he had finished his drink, he repacked the pack and noticed how dark it became, and he sat for a couple of minutes until his eyes adjusted to the darkness. When they did, he still couldn't see much, but the fungus at least outlined the tunnel walls and ceiling. The drink did at least wake him up and give him the energy to walk down the tunnel.

He walked on for about four hours before he was forced to take a rest, where the tunnel turned into a cave. It wasn't very big because he could still see the faint glow of the fungus, but up ahead, it appeared to be two tunnels leaving the area. One to the left and one to the right. He walked up to their entrances and sat down to ponder his plight. Once again, he opened his pack to get to the rations, and the glow from the eggs overwhelmed his eyesight until they could refocus. He unwrapped the eggs and selected the brightest one, a yellow egg that shone like an electric torch, and looked around the area while he ate his last energy bar. When his circumnavigation of the cave was complete, he decided to explore a short way into each tunnel. As far as he could tell, they were both pretty much the same but going apart by 45 degrees. The tunnels were obviously made by lava tubes, who knows how long ago, and they must have come from the Dragon Horn Mountains.

The trouble was, which tube to choose? They could both lead to dead ends. It could be very important which tube he chose, or they could both be good or bad, or both. He knew that he didn't have the energy to explore both of them and if he wasn't to die down here, he would soon need to find some food and water. He decided he would take the left fork, and as he walked in that direction, he noticed the yellow egg in his hand begin to glow even brighter. When he pointed the egg at the other tunnel, the egg lost its added brightness. The egg was trying to tell him something, but what? He closed his eyes and pointed the egg towards the left tunnel, then the right. When he pointed left, he could feel the love pour from the egg; when he pointed to the right, the feeling of love stopped. He pointed back to the left it began. Well, it seemed obvious to him that the eggs knew where they were going and had from the start, so who was he to stand in their way? So off they all went into the left tunnel!

He had not gone far, perhaps a mile, when the fungus stopped, and he was alone in the dark except for the egg, which seemed to glow even brighter. He trudged on, and after a while, he thought he could smell water up ahead; as he turned round the bend in the tunnel, he heard the sound of falling water and saw the light up ahead. After walking another quarter mile, he came into a vast cave and a large pool of water with a hole in the ceiling, allowing a broad beam of sunlight to enter. When he came to the water's edge, he sat the pack down and unstrapped the laser gun from his shoulder, and sat at the water's edge. He cupped his hands and brought out a hand full of the water and sniffed it, and when it smelled right, he took a small sip, and it tasted right, so he gathered up more and drank handful after handful. He took his water jug from the back of his pack and poured what little remained on the ground and began to rinse his jug, and then filled it to the brim with water. He then thrust his head into the water and began to wash his face and hands in the pool.

Afterward, he sat and wondered if he should eat his energy ration as it would leave him with just two left, but he decided to as the finding of the lake gave him a more hopeful outlook, and he was bone tired. He filed his cup from the lake and poured the half ration into the cup, and waited while it heated up and turned blue. As he sipped the hot liquid, he considered his fate along with the fate of the eggs. He had about three days before he would need to find some food. He briefly thought that he had another 12 meals wrapped in his spare shirt but quickly disregarded that thought. Maybe he could eat that fungus that grew on the ceiling. He assumed he would find some more in the tunnels when he left the cavern, as it apparently didn't like light. As for the dragons, as long as they didn't hatch out, they would be fine living off their egg yolk, but when they did, they would need a source of meat or at least protein. Still, he thought, one step at a time.

First, he needed to find a way out of this cavern. Were there any tunnels leading out, as the hole where the sunlight poured in was at least 200 feet above the lake? As he looked around, he saw that there was no way up to it. He would have to find another tunnel, but he needed a way to mark the tunnel he came out of so he would waste his time, and what little energy he had on it, so he gathered some rocks and made a pile of them before it.

When he had finished his energy drink, he rinsed out the cup and dipped out another cup full and drank it down, too, and then decided which way to walk around the cavern. The eggs seemed to know which way to go, so he pointed the egg again to the right and then to the left. This time the egg glowed the brightest to the right, so he picked up the pack, clipped the laser gun and cup back on the pack, and made his way to the right along the lake shore. After walking perhaps 300 yards, the cavern turned to his right, and after turning the corner, he heard something splashing in the water. He stopped and unhooked his gun and proceeded with caution along the shore.

He could hear the splashing and a curious voice, but who, or what, it was, was being blocked from his vision by a huge stalagmite thrusting up from the cave floor. When he came around the stalagmite, he saw a girl playing in the water with a baby dragon perched upon her shoulder, billing and cooing into her ear. As suddenly as he saw her, the dragon let out a high-pitched chirp, and she saw him standing there with the laser in one hand and the egg in the other!

She looked him over from head to toe and then said something in the Parlesian language, which he could understand about every fourth word. He didn't speak her language and could only speak broken Parlesian. So, he asked her if she could speak in Central Speak. Central Speak was a language that was developed by the 500 planets so that they could talk to one another. In that same strange accent, she said she did and asked him if he was the one, the "father of dragons?"

Father of dragons? He hadn't given it a lot of thought, but now that he did, he supposed it might be true. He had stolen the eggs to sell them for a fortune, or had he? When he thought of all that had happened, it seemed it was not so much his thought than it was theirs. He was a calculated, thoughtful person, but surely he should have known what would happen when he stole them. That several governments would move heaven and earth to get them back, perhaps even the central government? His actions were not something that he would normally do, so what did that mean? Apparently, he was just a pawn in a larger game! Eventually, he said that once he considered all the facts, he could be seen as the father of dragons.

She said that her name was Miri, and she was an exobiologist who had been drawn here to Parlesia but didn't know why until she stumbled upon a clutch of three dragon eggs. She was amazed that eggs seemed to talk to her and tell her what she must do. When they hatched, she realized that they had been controlling her long before she made the planet fall on Parlesia.

He introduced himself as Jamis Rabbin and proceeded to tell her his similar tale. As he did, two other little dragons flew up and landed, one on her shoulder and the other on her head. They cooed to her, and then all three looked at the egg in his hand. Seeing this, he sat down on the shore and opened his pack, and brought out the remaining 11 eggs, which made the three dragons very excited. While this happened, Miri walked toward Jamis and came out of the water. Jamis hadn't noticed that Miri was naked from the waist down and tried very hard to keep his eyes locked on hers.

She set the dragons down, and they all hopped to the eggs and began cooing to them. While they examined every egg, Miri took the time to put on a pair of shorts and her shoes and sat down opposite the clutch of eggs. Each egg had increased its glow which excited the little dragons even more. Jamis placed the egg he was holding back with the rest, and all three dragons ran to it and began sniffing and calling to it.

Miri said, "My dragons have told me many things about our quest. Did you notice that all three of them are males?"

"No, I hadn't," said Jamis. "My mind has been occupied looking at other things," he said to himself, as much as to her.

"Indeed," smiled Miri, knowing full well where his mind was at. "Oh, and did you know that all your dragons are females?" She continued.

"I see, said the blind man; now it's all beginning to make some sense," replied Jamis. "Why are we here, and where are we going," he continued.

"All I know is we're traveling to The Dragon Horn Mountains looking for someone or something called 'The Old One,'" Miri said.

"Funny, when I first entered the desert, I took a

bearing on those mountains, and for some reason, I started to head toward them, perhaps because they were the only thing visible above the desert, but I now suspect my 'children' may have had something to do with it," said Jamis wondering out loud.

"Don't feel bad, Jamis; I've already thrown away half of what I based my Ph.D. thesis on. I wouldn't bet against throwing away the rest of it before we are through," said Miri.

"What are you feeding your dragons?" Miri asked Jamis. "I'm almost out of food myself and have no idea what I can feed them when they hatch," continued Jamis.

"They have been feeding themselves, for the most part, most of the caves and tunnels are full of flying insects and birds, but I have given them a small part of my meat ration from time to time," she replied.

"How are your supplies holding out? I've got maybe two days rations left," said Jamis.

"You can share mine, as I have about a month's supply left, and we should be at the Dragon Horn's in two or three days if my calculations are correct," she offered.

"Well, if you have plenty, then I'll take you up on your generous offer," Jamis replied.

"If you have rested, then perhaps, we should move on," Miri said.

"I'm good to go, let me pick up my little darlings, and we'll be off," said Jamis. Then added, "How are you finding your way?"

"Like you, I've been following the dragons by following the glow of the eggs... When I come to a fork in the tunnel. I place my things near the tunnel they want us to take, so if you follow me, I'll take you there," Miri advised.

"Here's my camp; I perceived that we camped here in order to wait for your arrival because when I tried to walk away from this lake, they all took off and hovered over the entrance, and when I came back, they all took off, so I camped here waiting for their return. That was yesterday, and they only came back a few minutes before you came upon us. I was going to take my top off and go for a swim when I heard you approach," she explained.

After she had packed up her camp, he took the lead down the new tunnel; they hadn't gone but a little way when Miri said, "Your whole backpack is glowing quite brightly since we left the light of the cave."

"I suspect they've been doing that all along, but since we entered the dark, I've only become aware of it," said Jamis.

As they walked along, Jamis eventually told his story and his motives for stealing eggs and all that had happened to him since, and his conclusion that it was never his will but theirs behind everything.

Miri considered his story for a moment, then told her tale...

She had found the eggs in a market on Adigeon Prime, and as an exobiologist, she knew immediately what they were. Fortunately, the seller thought they were works of art without a clue as to what they were and their real worth. She thought they were unfertilized or dead and didn't give it much thought except for how they would look in her great room as decorations. She had gone back to work cataloging an ancient race that lived 10,000 years before but wasn't native to Adigeon Prime. It was several weeks later that she started having this desire to leave her work and make her way to Parlesia. At the time, it made perfect sense, but upon later reflection, she couldn't believe her actions. For no apparent reason, she left her important work behind and booked herself a tour of Parlesia's great polar dessert.

One night, for no apparent reason, she left the tour and went walking in the desert carrying the eggs and a sack full of supplies with her when she found herself sliding down a ramp into the darkness. When her eyes adjusted to the darkness, she could just barely make up two shapes; when she turned on the torch, she found the figures to be two huge Dragon Fleas, and she knew she was dead, but instead of ripping her to pieces, they parted and let her pass and began to push her in the right direction. As she looked ahead, she saw a tunnel and made a beeline for it; when she did, the Dragon Fleas stopped, then turned around and went back to the base of the slide. The next night just as she was slipping off to sleep, she heard the eggs cracking open, and eventually, three little dragons came forth and, within a few moments, unfurled their wings and came and landed around her face and made little cooing sounds; she made their sounds right back to them, and after a while, they settled down on her breasts and belly and went fast asleep, and after a while, she did too!

When she had finished her tale, they both fell silent, each thinking over what the other had said and adding both tales together and seeking out what each tale had surmised to their current situation. When they thought about it, they both came to the same conclusion; they were both tools of the dragons though they were pretty much opposites to begin with. She was a scholar, and he a slayer, but now both were on the same mission, but what was that mission?

After a time, Miri spoke up, breaking their spell.

"After considering our stories, I've concluded that the dragons have been controlling both of us from the very beginning to take them somewhere, but for what purpose I cannot currently grasp, but that knowledge may be the most important part of our quest," she exclaimed.

Jamis agreed by nodding his head and went back into deep thought as did. Miri...

Titania, the Fairy Queen, flew to the feet of the great dragon Esmeralda and bowed deeply, then got down on her knees and said...

"My queen, I bring you news about the babies. They are but two days walk away, and both carriers are now together. The males have hatched, and the females may hatch at any time."

"Thissss issss good," hissed Esmeralda. "You will continue to watch over them and ssssee to their ssssaftey. Go at oncccce and do ssssso," she continued.

Titania replied, "I will go at once and do so, my liege." She then arose, bowed deeply, took a few steps backward, and flew away back down the tunnel from whence she came.

This time it was Jamis who spoke. "If we are traveling with a purpose toward the unknown, my guess is we are taking them to another dragon to properly raise. And who knows better than I that all the dragons are supposed to be dead, but then we have obvious proof that isn't true. I'm having a bad feeling about this."

Miri spoke up, saying, "I have those bad feelings too. I remember what an old college professor said to me, and I quote, 'Don't meddle in the affairs of dragons, for you are crunchy and go good with wine.'"

Jamis thought for a moment and said, "That's funny; I once had a Ranger Captain who told me the very same thing," he exclaimed.

They both felt a chill and decided to break camp and walk down the next tunnel that continued their journey southward. Titania, who had been hovering a few yards away in the dark, landed and followed them down the tunnel, staying well back, but because of the glow emanating from Jamis' pack kept them barely in sight.

They walked for another 4 hours without saying anything and then took a break by a small stream that crossed their path. Miri took out her food rations and shared some with Jamis, saying, "Here, eat this; I have a feeling we'll need all of our strength in the days to come."

"Thanks," replied Jamis as he took the ration and began absent-mindedly feeding himself while watching the little dragons examining his backpack. The little blue dragon with the gold belly turned and looked his way, and he thought he heard the dragon telling him to open the backpack. He turned to question Miri, but she just smiled and nodded her approval without saying a word, so Jamis unbuckled the pack and set the eggs out in plain view. When he did this, all of the little dragons became excited and began flittering about just over the eggs making little cooing sounds.

"I think they're calling for the dragons inside the eggs to hatch," Miri said. "When mine hatched, the first one out almost at once began reacting the same way over the unhatched dragons, and it wasn't long before the other two hatched," Miri continued.

"Did you hear the blue dragon ask me to unbuckle my pack?" Asked Jamis.

"I didn't hear him so much as heard his thoughts," replied Miri.

"I heard sounds; I heard him telling me what he wanted to be done and in no uncertain terms either. It was more of a command than a request," said Jamis.

Miri started to reply when they both heard a cracking sound, and when they looked at the eggs, they could see one egg had clearly cracked; a moment later, it had cracked in two, and a bright golden dragon emerged and unwrapped its wings. This sent the already excited males to land all about her and begin to touch her and sniff her all over.

Meanwhile, down the tunnel, Titania got excited too, and it took all of her powers to stay away, but she did cut the distance between her and the dragons in half, again staying just out of sight. She would wait until the humans were asleep before calling the little ones to her.

Next came a bright purple dragon emerging from her shell, and all four of the dragons waited while she unfurled her wings before going over to greet her. Within the hour, all twelve eggs had hatched, and after flying around for a bit, they all settled down on both Jamis and Miri and went fast asleep, and after a while, both Jamis and Miri joined them. Titania waited a full hour before making herself known and whispered to the dragons, who awoke and flocked as one to her side. Although not a sound was heard, she talked to the little ones for almost an hour, and as one, they all lifted off and followed Titania down the tunnel toward Esmerelda!

Esmerelda had been asleep, but by the time they flew into her cave, she was wide awake and stepped off of her perch to greet them. They flew to her immediately, and she smiled and began to talk to them. They all perched at her feet and listened deeply to every word she said!

After a while, they all went to Titania and then returned to the sleeping Jamis and Miri and waited until the pair woke up. At first, they didn't notice the fairy, but when they did, they both jumped. Titania introduced herself and told them they had nothing to fear from her, and in fact, she was here to escort and protect them and the babies until they reached their destination just a few miles ahead. More than that, she did not say but waited until they had eaten their breakfast and had shared the crumbs with the babies, and were ready to travel.

When they left, the little ones stayed with Jamis and Miri and didn't flock with Titania led the way down the tunnel. With all the hatchlings glowing and pulsing all together, there was no need for any source of light as the tunnel seemed to reflect their light, and it was quite bright by tunnel standards. They walked for about an hour and then came out into a great cave lit by the sun high above. They walked another thousand yards, and when they came around a corner of the trail, they came face to face with Esmerelda.

Titania spoke up and introduced the dragon to Jamis and Miri. "This is my liege, the lady Esmerelda; she will see to the little ones," and to the dragon, she said. "These are the couriers who have been watching over the babies, my liege."

Esmerelda's bright red eyes looked at Jamis and Miri, her gaze feeling like it was looking deep into their souls. She then turned to Titania and said, "Yesssss thesssse two will do nicccely, well done Titania," she cooed. Then turned to Jamis and Mire, and instead of talking to them, she opened her mouth and sprayed them with her dragon fire; both were quite dead long before they hit the ground. To the little dragons, she said, "Eat your fill, my darlings, and I shall eat the rest." Humans are so nice and crunchy, but she'd need a keg of wine. Red wine, she thought, would do nicely!

THE TROUBLE WITH EARTHLINGS

"The trouble with Earthlings, how would you say it? Well, they're just too damn curious! They're always sticking their noses into everybody's business except their own. They're going to destroy the entire solar system someday unless they are stopped."

"Does the Senator have any suggestions?" A purple-clad Praetorian said as he stroked his magnificent tail.

"Yes, as a matter of fact, I do, General Steggisit. I would like his majesty and the council to consider the following suggestions. One: we give the Earth a final warning that unless it withdraws and keeps out of our section of space, we will destroy all human forms of life in the solar system. Two: if they don't immediately comply with our warning, we will do just that. Those General Steggisit are my suggestions."

"Isn't that a bit severe a punishment for what Earthlings did, Senator?"

Deep in his throne sat the king. Clad in his heavy battle harness and crown, absent-mindedly flicking just the tip of his tail to and fro as he listened to the debate of his council.

The junior Senator: from Sllewgh, the smallest of the seven cities of Mars, spoke up to ask the question on most of the Senator's minds, "What could the Earthlings have done this time to warrant their destruction?"

Just as the General was going to reply, the king awoke out of his lethargy and interrupted him by saying, "Yes, what indeed have they done this time? They have all but destroyed this planet. They've built their city while almost destroying the city of Vomisa. They daily pollute our air with their oxygen. One would almost think they were trying to change the atmosphere. What, pray to tell, have they done now?"

The general turned and, with a low sweeping bow, addressed his king. "Forgive me, sire. I thought you knew. One week ago, the Earthlings descended upon our colony on the first moon and utterly destroyed it. They managed to kill or capture the entire colony. They've taken all two hundred and fifty of them into their spacecraft and have begun to do horrible experiments on them. Apparently, your majesty, they radiated some of the bodies and then ate them. We only learned of this a few moments ago when a lone female child escaped and managed to send a report. That, your Highness, is what requires their destruction. All your majesty has to do is give the word, and I will personally see to it."

As the king sat listening to his general's report, his mouth slowly opened, and his lips pulled back, exposing row upon row of gleaming teeth. The king then spoke with an evil hiss in his voice, "Stand by General Steggisus; I may soon have need of you. Senator Camelus, if what General Steggisus says is true, then send forth messengers to the Earthling city and give them one rotation to pack up and leave or face the consequences. Go under the flag of the truce and carry no weapons or armor. We have been at peace for over 10,000 cycles, and I hesitate to break that peace, but enough is enough!"

Senator Cameleus bowed to the throne and quickly left with his aides to do the king's bidding. As he left, a hundred voices rang out as the Senate began arguing this point or that.

The king sat back to await the outcome of his courier message. The general din grew to a roar until the chamber door opened, and a bedraggled courier entered. All was quiet until the assembly gasped as one as they noticed that part of his tail was missing. He stumbled before the throne and bowed low before the king.

"Your majesty," he said as he gasped for breath.

"What are the Earthlings' reply, said the king?"

"Before we could even talk to them, we were attacked and all killed or captured except I, who managed to escape, sire," he replied.

"Not without certain sacrifices," mused the king with a smile that once again showed his row upon row of glistening teeth.

His smile quickly faded as he turned to face his council and said, "Yes, Senator Cameleus, we will indeed wipe these humans from the Solar System. Excuse me, gentlemen, but I must join my generals. Good day," and with a swish of his tail he was gone.

"Mars Probe One calling Phobos landing party, come in, over."

"This is Phobos landing party, over."

"How's the survival test going, Jim? Over."

"It's going great, Captain. We've run into the same life forms we found on Mars, sir, but not in as great a number. I'm afraid some of them were killed during capture, and I'm sorry to report that some of the carcasses were cleaned and microwaved by some of the hungrier members of the crew. They're currently being watched over by Doc, but they seem to be all right. Over."

"Found any little green men, Commander? Over."

"No sir, just these little green or purple lizards. Over."

"Found any intelligent life forms, Jim? Over."

"No, Captain, just the lizards and some red moss. Over."

"Well, pack up Jim and bring your expedition back to Bradbury City over."

"Yes, sir. We'll dock at the orbiting station in six hours. Phobos landing party, over and out."

First Officer James Campbell looked up into space where the Earth was but a bright blue speck. To think mankind had come this far in space in just the sixty years since Apollo. He smiled to himself and continued gazing at the Earth as it, along with Mars Probe One and all of her crew, disappeared in a blinding flash of light!

CHRISTOPHER RABBIT'S BIG EASTER ADVENTURE

Christopher Rabbit was one confused little bunny. Not only had Christopher Rabbit not listened to his mother when she warned him about staying out of Mr. MacGregor's garden, but also about staying away from Mr. MacGregor's tool shed! Oh, if only Christopher Rabbit had listened to his mother!

After a delicious salad from Mr. MacGregor's vegetable patch, Christopher Rabbit had gone hippity-hop right into Mr. MacGregor's tool shed to sleep off his esurient orgasm, where he curled up under a tarp by a bale of straw and went fast asleep.

Christopher Rabbit slept and slept and slept. He slept right through Mr. MacGregor entering the shed. He slept right through Mr. MacGregor, pulling the tarp off his latest invention, the "Zeppelin Tube," or "Z-tube." But when Mr. MacGregor, dressed in his finest radiation suit, turned on the Z-tube, Christopher Rabbit awoke rather abruptly from a very pleasant dream concerning the Hare sisters, Gladys and Gloria, a bottle of ranch dressing, and a couple of rather large carrots, into a nightmare scene lit by purple light and a strange feeling that pulsed through him in waves of pure energy. After Christopher Rabbit knew the effects of the Z Tube "first paw," was when "Christopher Rabbit's Big Easter Adventure" really began! ...

Ten thousand suns exploded into a black swirling funnel into which Christopher Rabbit was thrust around and around the blue event horizon. Faster and faster, he was spun until everything went red, then blue, then white, then black...

"Oh, Mr. Rabbit... Mr. Rabbit, do wake up," said a rather exquisitely dressed Hedgehog named Gerald as he gently slapped a rather-startled Christopher Rabbit back to reality.

"Oh, Mr. Rabbit," Gerald said again as he backhanded a now wide-awake, very confused, and sputtering little bunny. Whap!

"Please, Mr. Hedgehog; stop hitting me; I'm awake; I'm awake," cried Christopher Rabbit. "Indeed, you are," said Gerald as he slapped Christopher Rabbit one last time for good measure! Whap!

"Welcome to Easterland," said Gerald. "I assume that you've come for the job?"

Massaging his well-slapped cheeks, Christopher Rabbit cringed a bit and asked Gerald, "What job?"

"Why, the Easter Bunny job, of course," replied Gerald!

"My word," said Christopher Rabbit. "I always thought that the Easter Bunny story was a fairy tale!"

"No, indeed not," said Gerald. "The Easter Bunny has always been the sign of Spring virility, and Randy Rabbit, our last Easter Bunny, just died after eating a couple of Viagra-laced carrots and stumbling into the Hare Sister's apartment for a wild weekend. He died with a smile on his face and left two very satisfied ladies; so, we need a new Easter Bunny for this Easter, and I'm betting it's you," said Gerald, quite assuredly.

"How can you tell if I'm the one? What would I have to do? When would I have to start? Will I get to meet the Hare Sisters, too? What's it pay; is there per diem, too?" Asked a stammering Christopher Rabbit.

Suddenly, Gerald knew what he had to do to calm the overly excited bunny and immediately began to backhand the little bunny -- once, twice, and a third time for good measure. Whap! Whap! Whap!

When Christopher had calmed down, Gerald said, "There is one who can answer your many questions and who will know if you're the true Easter Bunny."

"Who's that?" Asked Christopher.

"Why, the great horned owl Aristotle, who else? He lives two days' walk from here -- if anybody knows if you're the one, it's him. He lives in a great tree in the middle of 'Hero's Death' Woods, deep in the dark forest. I shall put you on the right path, but you must beware; there are things in the forest -- things that you do not want to meet in the dark," whispered Gerald with an evil-looking grin.

This sent shivers down the little bunny's spine and

started to give him second thoughts. Before he could have those thoughts, Gerald spun him around in the right direction: and, taking one of his exquisite boots, he brought it up smartly into Christopher Rabbit's rump -- WHAP! Which sent the now-scurrying little bunny hippity-hop-pity down the old bunny trail and into the deep, dark, dank, scary woods!

Just as Christopher entered the forest, Alfred the Ferret peeked out behind a tree where he had been eavesdropping on Christopher and Gerald and broke down in gales of laughter as he high/low slapped Gerald's hand, exclaiming, "The great horned owl Aristotle; that's just an old wives' tale! We both know the only thing that poor little bunny is going to find in 'Hero's Death' woods is LeRoy, the Dire Wolf. That's 500 pounds of savage, bone-crunching hell! Aristotle, oh, please," chuckled Alfred, "that poor, stupid little bunny."

With a practical look on his face, Gerald said, "I send LeRoy the occasional would-be Easter Bunny, and he leaves us alone here -- seems fair, and besides, I warned Christopher Rabbit that there were things in those woods that you do not want to meet in the dark, and that certainly describes LeRoy, does it not? C'est la vie, bunny!"

It had been a bright and sunny day, just approaching the noon hour; but after walking for about ten minutes, it now looked to be about dusk; and when he climbed a hill and looked behind him, it was still bright sunshine in the little dot of light where he'd entered the forest. I wonder what it will be like at midnight, thought Christopher and that thought sent a shiver down his spine. At about the time that he realized it was getting really dark for early afternoon, he also noticed that it was perfectly quiet in these woods. When he entered the woods, there were plenty of birds singing, with little animals scurrying here and there; but now it was silent - - not even wind got in here to make a noise. This can't be good, thought Christopher Rabbit! And it wasn't good. Something far off in the deepest part of the forest was deep in sleep, reliving a particularly bloody slaughter of his last victim, a would-be Easter Bunny named Richard Rabbit. Even though he was in the deepest part of REM sleep, LeRoy was becoming more and more aware of Christopher. His subconscious made a mental note to look Christopher up at the stroke of Midnight and went back to its relived savagery! At the same time, many miles away from the Dire Wolf's den, Christopher Rabbit felt a shiver go up and down his spine.

"Well, what is this thing that I've found?" Said a mysterious voice from somewhere overhead.

"I'm not a thing; I'm a rabbit; to be precise, I'm Christopher Rabbit!" Christopher Rabbit exclaimed to the darkness overhead. "Who, who are you?" He then timidly asked.

"Rabbit," exclaimed the voice overhead. "I love Rabbit," said the mysterious voice. "In fact, Mr. Rabbit, I'd like to ask you to join us for dinner!" "Oh, yes, dinner, dinner, yes, dinner, dinner, dinner, dinner," echoed another dozen voices high up in the tree.

"I'm not sure," said Christopher. Realizing that he

was getting a little hungry, Christopher asked, "What are you having for dinner?"

The first voice asked the others, "What shall we have for dinner tonight, my children? We could have that old favorite, Hasenpfeffer, braised in a red wine gravy flavored with bacon, shallots, currant jelly, and herbs. Of course, nothing beats a good old Louisiana Back-bay Bayou Bunny Bordelaise, a la Antoine; am I right? Oh, and Mr. Rabbit, I'm Cornelius! Cornelius, the Great Green Tree Spider, Mr. Rabbit," said Cornelius, as he lowered himself into Christopher Rabbit's view, as did dozens and dozens of other Great Green Tree Spiders, both large and small. Or, at least, Christopher would have seen them, had he still been there; but because Christopher's skin had begun to crawl like it did whenever something dangerous might be about, so when Christopher Rabbit heard the word "Hasenpfeffer," he went hippity hoppity right back down the bunny trail -- at full speed. Praying feet don't fail me now!

Spiders are fairly dumb; but it didn't take them too long to realize that dinner was running away at a fairly good clip; and if they didn't hurry, he'd make his escape across the great divide! So, young and old, big and small, they began running along the various spider paths from tree to tree to tree, all calling out in their low-pitched voices, "Christopher, Christopher, we want to have you for dinner!"

Christopher Rabbit ran and ran and ran and then ran some more. He ran faster and farther than he had ever run before, but the spiders' chants kept getting louder and louder, sounding now like they were almost overhead. Just when it seemed it was hopeless, he saw a small dot of light ahead and, with the last of his strength, plunged from the darkness into a new sunrise and a clear space of about 200 yards between the forest, running as far as the eye could see in both directions.

Christopher Rabbit lay on his back in the field and desperately tried to catch his breath: and, above and behind him, Cornelius jumped up and down, yelling great curses at Christopher Rabbit as the little bunny was beyond his reach; he was a dozen yards from the nearest tree, and Great Green Tree Spiders never leave the treetops, except to slide down on a web strand to catch a meal; so, in case of danger, they could climb back and be way out of range. Worse yet, the direction he was traveling when he crossed the field and fell down gasping was toward the land of the "Great Blue Tree Spiders" and their King, the dreaded Shadrack! Shadrack and Cornelius never ever got along, and Cornelius would rather see Christopher Rabbit escape than fall into the eight hands of the evil Shadrack!

By now, Christopher Rabbit had caught his breath but was far too tired to get up and move onward, so he just lay there as the sun rose and soon fell fast asleep.

Two hundred yards back in the woods, the great Dire Wolf sat watching Christopher Rabbit napping--had he been here 15 minutes earlier, Christopher Rabbit would have been a resounding burp, echoing through the woods, but Dire Wolfs never go out in the sunlight: so, eventually, LeRoy, too, succumbed to sleep as the morning moved onward.

THE SPIDERS DIDN'T BOTHER LeRoy; catching and eating a little bunny was one thing, but catching and eating an angry, snarling, 500-pound Dire Wolf was another! So, Cornelius and his tribe went back to catching tree frogs, caterpillars, and birds!

Christopher Rabbit awoke with a start as a shadow passed over him; even in a tired sleep, Christopher Rabbit knew death from above when it crossed his closed eyes. Christopher Rabbit nervously checked the sky to figure out which way to run, but it was only a man-machine and not the red-tailed hawk that he feared. Eventually, his heart stopped pounding; and he realized he was quite hungry and looked around the meadow for something to eat and found some lovely Polk salad and dandelions, which filled his belly up quite full; and over by where the woods began again was a little stream with ice cold, flowing water, and Christopher Rabbit stopped to drink his fill and then attend to his toilet. He washed his face and paws, brushed his whiskers, and then brushed his teeth with a thistle. He then brushed off his velvet jacket and picked a briar off his top hat as he wanted to be at least presentable to the great horned owl, Aristotle.

He was soon off and back into the woods, which didn't seem so overgrown as the other side had; you could, from time to time, see the sun overhead. It was about noon when the forest closed up and became quite as dark as the other one; suddenly Christopher Rabbit's skin began to crawl, and he thought he heard a little deep spider voices: so, off he went hoppity hop at a frightful pace; and didn't slow down until the sun had set and the gloomy dark became almost total darkness. Christopher Rabbit became aware of that exact time through telepathy because that was the moment that LeRoy awoke with a howl and began to gallop after the bunny. A few seconds later, he had crossed the meadow at full speed, running down the very path that Christopher Rabbit took. "Easter Bunny, Yum, Yum," thought LeRoy, and he let out another bloodcurdling, howling roar!

Christopher Rabbit had stopped at a lovely patch of wild carrots and strawberries and had eaten his way about halfway through it when he heard LeRoy's roar and stood straight up and began hopping off toward the center of the forest--but only after loading his pockets with baby carrots!

Christopher Rabbit had about an eight-hour head start, but a couple of hours later LeRoy had halved the distance, and even though Christopher Rabbit began running in earnest, at that point, because the Dire Wolf had let out a mighty roar that even Christopher Rabbit could hear -- LeRoy was gaining ground, and he knew it!

As they approached the center of the woods and the area known as the 'Hero's Death,' the forest canopy began to thin out to where that brilliant full moon could penetrate to the ground and cause shadows -- not a good thing with a Dire Wolf on your tail! Suddenly, up ahead, Christopher Rabbit saw the biggest tree that he had ever seen. From a huge base, many, many hops around it soared into the air, where it split into four great limbs that soared even higher into the sky. Such a tree, thought Christopher Rabbit, could hide a hundred hawks, a thousand hawks, and at such a thought, Christopher Rabbit came to a screeching halt and stood shaking before it. Then he remembered that Aristotle lived in such a tree, and at last, his journey was over; and he walked into the clearing surrounding the great tree and timidly said, "Oh, Aristotle... Please, Mr. Aristotle, might we have a word?" Christopher Rabbit thought he might have seen movement high up near the top of the tree, so he cried out a little louder, "Please, Mr. Aristotle, can you help me?"

A deep and disturbing voice behind Christopher Rabbit said, "He can't hear you, Christopher: there is no great horned owl named Aristotle; it was all just a lie to make you my dinner, little bunny," said LeRoy, and he made lip-smacking sounds and rubbed his belly while smiling, thus showing Christopher Rabbit his mouth full of razor-sharp fangs. The Dire Wolf stood looking into the air, stroking his chin as if in deep thought, then turned to Christopher and said in a whisper, "I think I'll start by biting off your head and eating it! Rabbit heads are so nice and crunchy, hmmm, yum, come here, Mr. Bunny...."

As LeRoy reached for Christopher Rabbit, it seemed Christopher Rabbit was frozen under the Dire Wolf's spell and couldn't move a muscle. LeRoy sprinted the few yards between himself and Christopher Rabbit, and just as he was about to wrap his claws around Christopher Rabbit, another set of claws grabbed Christopher Rabbit and took him away, while at the same time, something hit the Dire Wolf hard and sent him rolling end-over-end for about 50 yards. When he stopped rolling, his head was ringing; and he put both paws over his ears to stop it, and then he looked around for the truck that had hit him. Only then he saw the great horned owl Aristotle with Christopher Rabbit in one clawed hand, flying higher and higher into the night, over the trees and out of sight! Just before he disappeared, Aristotle said to LeRoy, "Gerald sends his regards!" LeRoy, hearing this, let out a roar that shook the countryside!

When Aristotle had plucked him from the jaws of death, Christopher Rabbit had fainted dead away. Had he remained awake for the flight, he would have seen that Aristotle was flying him back the way he had come -- to where he had been when first he had awakened. About an hour after dawn, the great horned owl gently landed on one foot and gently deposited Christopher Rabbit on the ground with the other. Christopher Rabbit awoke to look up into the wise eyes of the old owl. He was no longer afraid but felt safe and so asked, "Mr. Aristotle, am I an Easter Bunny?"

"I thought about as much," said the great owl as much to himself as to Christopher Rabbit. "You are indeed the Easter Bunny, my fine, young friend," said Aristotle, almost cooing, to Christopher Rabbit. However, when Aristotle looked up and over to where Gerald stood looking very nervous, gallons of flop sweat soaking his fine clothes, he said in a very different, deep, dark voice that seemed to echo, "Get over here, Gerald! NOW!"

Gerald, upon hearing this first, almost jumped out of the skin, and then made a beeline to stand in front of the great owl. Gerald was a lot closer to Aristotle than he'd like to be, and he couldn't take his eyes off that beak -- oh, that beak! Aristotle saw what was going through Gerald's mind and said, "I should nip off your head and feed it to my babes. Every creature in Easterland knows that there is no test, no quest! Everybody knows that any rabbit that makes it to Easterland is the Easter Bunny. Now give him his magic basket, his ID badge, and get him to the bunny trail at once as tomorrow is the Equinox; and then it's only 11 days to Easter, and with a few billion Easter eggs to deliver, he'd better get at it."

Gerald rather sheepishly got the basket and handed it to Christopher Rabbit without ever looking him in the eye, muttering how sorry he was for his little "joke." As Gerald slinked away, Christopher Rabbit examined the Easter Basket. On the outside, it was a regular Easter basket, nothing really special; but when he looked inside, he saw a most amazing machine that held but a single egg; but what it was somehow attached to was a truly awe-inspiring sight! For around and around and around the center of the basket spun a black hole, and around its event horizon spun a billion trillion eggs, each with different colors and designs. When Christopher Rabbit removed the egg from the top of the basket, another egg came up from down below to take its place.

Christopher Rabbit gave the first egg to Gerald and the next one to Alfred the Ferret, who came out of hiding when he realized there was something in it for him to eat. When Christopher Rabbit turned to Aristotle to offer him one, the great horned owl shook his head and said, "No, thanks, Christopher; I'm thinking of having a helping of Hedgehog and Ferret! Now, Gerald, show Christopher where the bunny trail begins; and be quick about it."

Gerald asked Christopher Rabbit to follow him just over the hill, and there it was – you could hardly miss it. The trail was covered with jellybeans in every color of the rainbow, and then some, and they all seemed to be glowing from within.

As Christopher Rabbit looked over the scene, Aristotle rose into the air and called to Christopher Rabbit in his gentle voice, "Good luck, my little friend; we're all counting on you, and I know you won't let us down!" Then he turned and flew low over Gerald and Alfred and said in his other voice, "Although I should eat you for what you've done, I won't. Besides, it wouldn't be fair to poor, old LeRoy; I snatched the bunny from out of his jaws; so I know he must be hungry; and as I flew away, I mentioned your name, Gerald. That really seemed to upset LeRoy, so, my guess is he should be here by Midnight tonight. Midnight tomorrow, at the latest!" And with one last dive inches above their heads, Aristotle was gone.

Christopher Rabbit was soon hopping down the bunny trail, leaving a colorful egg under every tree and bush in the entire world. It was hard work; he never thought he could do it on time, but he did; and when he finally got home to his family's warren, they all celebrated his great achievement. The mayor made a speech, and he was given many awards; and then, at one particularly boring party, he looked around -- and suddenly there, in the flesh, were the Hare Sisters! And even better, they were coming his way! The next thing he knew, they had dragged him away from a perfectly awful party and back to their apartment to an epicurean feast, ending with a bottle of ranch dressing, a couple of rather large carrots, and the sisters. And unlike Randy Rabbit, Christopher didn't "need no stinking,' Viagra-stuffed carrots" and easily survived the lost weekend.

Then Mr. MacGregor turned off the Z-tube, covered the machine, and then left the shed while Christopher Rabbit snapped awake under the tarp beside the bale of straw in Mr. MacGregor's shed. It had only been a dream. Christopher Rabbit was heartbroken; it had been the best and worst time of his life, and it had only been a dream -- it had never happened, oh, heavy sigh!

It was just then that Christopher Rabbit's mother, Rhonda Rabbit began calling her children for supper, and Christopher Rabbit trudged along back to his home. "Oh well, I guess Mother was right; I should go into Chartered Accountancy -- no adventures for the likes of me," Christopher Rabbit moaned.

It was just then there was a knock on the door, and Mrs. Rabbit answered it, speaking for a moment to someone, then closed the door and came into the kitchen. She was carrying the Easter Basket, "Gloria Hare just dropped this off; she said you'd left this in her apartment, and she wondered where you wandered off to?" Christopher Rabbit was all smiles from that day forward!

MRS. WEATHERBY'S CLIENTELE

Elizabeth Weatherby felt the warmth of the setting sun upon her eyelids as she came out of the fourth stage of REM sleep. She lay all warm and cozy for a minute and then awoke with a start, she was late, and it didn't pay for her to be late with her special clientele.

She sprang naked from her bed and made a beeline for her shower. Fifteen minutes later, she had finished her toilet and had run back to her bedroom to hurriedly dress herself. As she locked her front door, she noticed that the sun was just above the horizon, so she breathed a sigh of relief as she realized that she wasn't as late as she had supposed herself to be. She would have time to stop for a large coffee and a bear claw to go before she got to work; at least, that was something.

Soon she was driving down the familiar cul-de-sac to her clinic, which sat on the end of the street it was the only building on the street. There was a parking lot on either side of the building, and in this case, five cars were parked, four of which belonged to her staff and one late donor. The donor was busily counting his money and didn't notice Mrs. Weatherby as she drove by and around to the back of the building to her parking space and the door to her office.

She entered her office, put her purse down, then walked through the opposite door and entered the clinic's hallway. Past the laboratories, and refrigerators rooms, into the outer lobby where her staff was awaiting her. They were her three nurses and her secretary, who handed her the daily report sheets. She glanced at the totals and turned and set them on their way, and then locked the front door behind them. She left the lobby and entered the hallway, and locked the steel door where the lobby met the hallway. She pushed a button that made the sign that said the "Weatherby Clinic" drop into the roof and turned on the bright red neon sign that popped up in its place that said, "Life Stream Laboratories." She then pushed the button that raised a bulletproof glass shield that separated the lobby from her station, where she dispensed the blood with a spinning circular box in the center.

By now, the sun had set, and the afterglow was beginning to fade away; it wouldn't be long now. She clipped on the 45 calibers Smith & Wesson that fired wooden stakes instead of lead and awaited her special clientele. She never needed the gun, but her dear departed husband, Richard, who got a little too friendly with a Upior, could have certainly used one. There were very few Upior among her clientele, mostly your average vampire and most perfect gentlemen and ladies. They knew a good thing when they found one.

The Upior in question met a grisly end when attacked and ripped slowly to pieces by a pack of were-wolves, whose leader was the old silver back, Charles, whom she had adopted as her lover with the death of Richard. Charles had watched her shoot a wooden bullet through Richard's heart as he returned from the dead. In her position, it was nice to have a pack of werewolves at your beck and call!

It wasn't long before she heard the night call door-bell; the door was invisible to most human eyes. She buzzed them through as she sat behind the counter and awaited their arrival. Her first clientele was a pair of brothers who were brought over by their own mother at the beginning of the 12th century CE. They came in on an average of twice a week and ordered two warm bottles of B positive and six cold to go, a typical order for which they paid $2,000. Her rates went from $100 a bottle for O positive, $150 a bottle for O negative to $3,000 for B negative and $5,000 a bottle for AB nega-tive for a full blood, and O plasma could be had if you were down and out, for $50 a bottle.

She took the brother's money, and as they took their time sipping the warm blood, she put the other six bottles of B positive into a carrier for them to take home and drink at their leisure.

The next to arrive was a pair of teenage girls doing all the things that teenagers do, except that these teenage girls were 400 years old. They both ordered two bottles of O positive, two warm and two cold to go. It was only after they had paid for the blood and turned to leave that Elizabeth took her hand off the Smith & Wesson!

The brothers drank their bottles down and followed the girls out the side door, leaving their empties in the spinning circular box as they grabbed their carrier. Elizabeth grabbed the two empties and placed them in a carrier sitting on a shelf by her knees.

Her next customer was a man dressed in a $3,000 suit and $1,000 shoes. He called himself "The Count," and for all, she knew, he might be a Count. He ordered a six-pack of AB Negative, one warm and five cold to go, and paid the $30,000 in $100 dollar bills. When she counted the money, she found two things, one, when she counted, it came to $35,000, and two they were all in sequential order. She assumed that they were stolen, but for an extra four grand profit, she would look the other way. At the cost of $1000, she would launder the money for the Count, and everyone was happy!

She scanned the parking lot, and when no one was seen, she clicked on the back in five minutes sign, which wouldn't start a five-minute countdown until someone approached the door or she turned it off. She went back to her office and took a bathroom break, and then grabbed what was left of her bear claw and made her way back to the front. No one was by the door, so she turned off the sign and took the empties back to the cleaning station, and returned just as a pair of couples buzzed for entry to the building.

There was a man and a woman, and two women who approached the counter holding hands. These were all new customers, as both couples took their time to read the menu before placing their orders. The man and the woman order six bottles of O negative, two warms and four cold to go. The ladies ordered 8 bottles of O positive, two warm, and 6 to go. Elizabeth typed the order into the computer, and the orders soon popped up beside her. Seeing that these were newbies, she collected their money before dispensing the blood. Both couples wanted to know what her hours were, and she wanted to know how they found out about her service. They chatted pleasantly while she put their cold blood into containers for them to take with them.

And so, the night went. About a half hour before dawn, all her customers left, and she turned off her nighttime signs and brought her daytime sign back up. She took the empties back to the cleaning station and, after counting her money again, put the totals on her laptop computer and into "the book." She separated the Count's money from the rest and put it in a separate pile in the safe. She then typed a code into her desktop computer, and the laptop, book, and safe disappeared into a vault on her floor. By the time she was finished filling in her sales for her secretary, it was time to open the front door for her staff to enter. They were all sitting in their cars waiting for her to open the door and soon entered the building and went to their workstations while Elizabeth had a few words with her secretary before grabbing her purse and coat and heading out for breakfast. So went Elizabeth's day.

When Richard was alive, he had handled the clinic at night, and with her MBA from Harvard, she handled the finances. The Counts' $35,000 would soon find its way to an offshore banking account in the Cayman Islands, where it would be washed and sent back to her via the local farmers' bank and then to her vault.

Any extra blood they took in, which was usually O positive and O negative, was sold to the local hospitals at the going rate plus 20%.

By the time she got to her restaurant, she was all but starving as the bear claw had worn off hours ago, so she had her typical breakfast of a three-egg omelet, a small steak, hashbrowns, toast, and coffee. As she was finishing her second cup of double Espresso and looked up, there sat Charles smiling at her from across the table. She tried hard not to flinch as Charles seemed to appear out of thin air! Werewolves were like that!

Charles asked her what her plans were for today, and since she had none, Charles invited her over to his new place to show her where it was and what it was like. Charles followed her home and, after she had changed into a new outfit,, joined him in his Bentley for the trip up into the hills. There, sitting on an overlook, was a small castle of about 25000 square feet with a tower on the four corners. It was surrounded by a 20 ft high wall with iron gates opening to allow them entrance. The house set back about a hundred feet from the walls and had a circular driveway. Charles pulled up before the double doors that allowed admittance, got out and ran around to Elizabeth's side, and opened her door.

Charles pushed a key fob, and the two doors swung out, and he guided Elizabeth inside into the foyer, where two staircases circled down to greet them; in the center between them was an elevator. To either side of the foyer were rooms leading off in different directions. He walked over to the elevator and took them up to the fifth floor, where the door opened to a large living room with an even larger bedroom on either side. He entered the bedroom on the left side and took a seat on the couch, and bade Elizabeth to join him. She kicked off her shoes and joined Charles on the couch, where they immediately went into an embrace. An hour later, they went into the shower, after which Charles sent her to bed to get some sleep while promising to get her up in time for dinner and work.

Elizabeth closed her eyes, and suddenly, it was eight hours later when Charles awoke her with a tender kiss. She rose and pulled Charles into bed for a long loving cuddle, followed by another love-making session, followed by another shower. After she had got dressed, Charles took her down two floors and into a dining room where dinner was soon arriving. She finished her fine meal with another two double Espressos. She glanced at her watch, and Charles nodded when they went through the double doors; the Bentley was waiting, and off they went back to Elizabeth's house, where Charles left her with a kiss as she went and changed her clothes and jumped into her car and drove off to work stopping only for her large coffee and bear claw!

Again, she parked behind the building and made her way through the backdoor and into her office. She visited her restroom, then typed in the code from her desktop, and the safe, book, and laptop rose from beneath the floor and into their upright position. She then met up with her secretary, who gave her the daily report sheets. After scanning the report, she noticed that two new clients had sold her two pints of AB negative which were always in short supply, and with her smile, her secretary Linda added that she had given them a special enticement; an extra hundred dollars more than the listed price, to keep them coming back. This was standard procedure to ensure a steady supply of AB negative as it was a little over half the cost if they had to buy it from a blood bank or hospital.

Elizabeth then sent her staff home and got the building ready for her customers. She returned to her office and drank half of Espresso and ate half of the bear claw, and returned to the front to await her first customers. She didn't have long to wait. While she was scanning her blood supply on the computer, her first customer rang the doorbell and was buzzed through.

It was Aristotle, a boy who looked to be no more than nine or ten years old but was, in reality, over 3,000 years old. He ordered one warm bottle of B positive and seven cold to go, which was his typical order for which he paid $2,000. Next came the two 400-year-old teenage girls. Again, they both ordered two bottles of O positive, two warm and two cold to go, and so the night went until it was about an hour before sun-up when she buzzed through first a female and then a male. He let her order first, and she took her order of a warm bottle of B positive and seven cold to go, for which she paid $2,000. In a blink of an eye, he staked her through the heart and made a dash for the door with her bottles. He made it through the first door, but the outer door was locked, and a second later, so was the inner door. Had he looked up, he would have seen the blanket of silver mesh chain that fell on him from the ceiling and pinned him to the floor. Elizabeth picked up her 45 calibers Smith and Wesson with the oak-pointed bullets and let herself out of the left hallway and then into the right hallway, where she shot him into a pile of goo with one shot from the gun. She would have to call her cleaners!

She turned off the "Life Stream Laboratories" sign and turned on the "Weatherby Clinic" sign, and awaited the arrival of her cleaners. In under fifteen minutes, they were there, and she let them in through the front door. Half the crew started immediately in the lobby while the other wrangled the silver mesh blanket off him and put it in a large bag, and removed it from the building; they would take it back to their shop and steam clean it and then bring back and rehang it well before the sun went down. Elizabeth waited until they had finished the lobby and had started on the right hallway before she let the day shift in.

She took her secretary aside and explained what had happened and told her to expect the cleaners to return the chain mesh blanket this afternoon and let them in and out through the vampire's door so anyone in the lobby wouldn't know. She picked up the 8-pack of blood and took it back to the refrigerator room and put the cold bottles back into the machine and poured the warm one down the sink, and placed the container into the scrubbing machine! Thankfully this would pay for the cleaners. She then returned to her office and removed the spent cartridge from the gun, and replaced it with a new one which she glazed a bit on some garlic juice before loading it into her gun. She inspected and counted the money before placing it into the safe and lowering the safe, "book," and laptop into the floor. It was only after everything was back to normal did she feel a shiver run down her spine.

After breakfast, on her way out of the restaurant, she noticed the full moon rising, which meant Charles wouldn't be by as the pack spent the night and day of the full moon locked in their rooms on the fourth floor of the castle. The pack could turn into werewolves on any day, but on the full moon, they couldn't keep from going just a bit crazy when they turned, and to keep things on the down low and under control, they were locked into their "full moon" rooms. She'd see Charles tomorrow, so she went home and got some needed rest.

She managed to get to work a bit early as she wanted to do some things before sunset. She wanted to see if the banquet of silver chain mesh had been cleaned and rehung properly and that the area was spotless before she went over to their shop and paid them cash for their services tomorrow morning. No checks, credit, or debit cards leave a trail for the government to follow. Her cleaners completely understood and were happy with the cash.

After running her inspection and talking with Linda, she retreated to her office with today's figures, then called the cleaners for their bill and entered the figures in the laptop and the "book." She then worked on her mainframe computer until the alarm bell sounded, marking 15 minutes to sunset. She left her office and sent her staff home while she prepared the lobby for tonight's visitors. She hadn't long to wait as 5 minutes after the sun had set, the familiar black limousine pulled up, and out stepped the Count and rang the doorbell!

As usual, he ordered a six-pack of AB Negative, one warm and five cold to go, and paid the $30,000 again in $100 dollar bills. When he smiled at her, he looked a bit like Bela Lugosi, but when the smile faded, not so much. He left the building and drove away. When he did so, two more cars pulled up. The first to enter was the new lesbian couple who ordered eight bottles of O positive, two warm and 6 to go. They paid the $800 before she gave them their bottles. After the other night, she took nothing for granted.

The two 12th-century brothers were next and ordered their typical order, i.e., two warm bottles of B positive and six cold to go, for which they paid $2,000. And so, the evening went on until just before dawn, a man approached the building and was buzzed through. He was a newbie and took his time reading the menu, too much time as the bell announcing daylight rang. He then ordered eight bottles of O negative, one warm and seven cold to go, and paid the $1200 dollars; the trouble was the sun was almost above the horizon. Elizabeth gave him the warm blood and told him to go back down the hallway and through the door at the end, which led into a sunless room with a couch and a coffin. She told him when the sunset, she would tell him, and he could pick up the rest of his order. When the building was being built, allowances were made for just such an emergency, but as far as she knew, this was the first time it was ever used.

When her staff arrived, she took Linda aside and told her of their guest and then returned to her office and made a note on her laptop and sent it, the "book" and safe, into the vault, and off she went for a hearty breakfast!

After her breakfast, she had expected to look up and see Charles, but he was nowhere in sight. She got into her Cadillac and noted it was only on a quarter charge, so she pulled into her garage and plugged it in. When she walked onto her back porch, she noted Charles was sitting on the lounge. She had glanced at the back porch as she drove by, and there was no one there! Somehow, she was not surprised as werewolves were like that! She opened the back door, and he followed her in.

She put down her purse and coat and turned into his arms for a kiss, then made small talk about her shift as he told her about his day and night of the full moon, of how the children reacted to the lockdown. She hadn't realized that there were children in the pack! Two couples had "pups." One had a son, and the other had twin girls, and the girls, like teenagers everywhere, were a little upset about the lockdown. She told him of her 400-year-old teenage vampires, and they commiserated about children. Just as they were about to go to bed, her phone rang; it was the office calling to say there had been a police raid, and they needed her to come to the clinic.

Now what, she thought, as she called her attorney and went and changed her clothes before kissing Charles goodbye and promising to call him when she knew what was happening and then made her way to work.

She pulled into her parking spot behind the building and entered her office. Sitting at her desk, trying to unlock her desktop computer, was a uniformed police-woman. She walked past the desk and down the hallway passed the blood rooms and cleaning station to the front lobby where the DA and county sheriff, and others were questioning Linda and the nurses. All of whom were not cooperating but waiting for her attorneys to arrive. She recognized the DA and went directly to him. To receive and read the search warrant.

As she did, her attorneys filed in and surrounded the DA and Sheriff with a thousand questions of their own. Her personal attorney took the search warrant and read it, then told Elizabeth what this was really all about was that the DA was running for state Attorney General and had promised the sheriff he'd take him along if he helped him make something out of this Weatherby Clinic case. On a tip, someone had told him that all was not as it seemed at the clinic, and it was worth looking into. The "tip" had come from the county's other blood bank, and the DA, who at this point was grasping at straws in his campaign, had jumped at the chance.

The governor, the state attorney general, a state senator, and a US Senator all knew of what Elizabeth was doing and approved of it. The DA was saying there had been several murders in the area, and with the tip, he was just investigating to see if the clinic was somehow involved and if we were innocent. Would I unlock my mainframe and the lobby computer? Her attorney advised against it, but Elizabeth assured him that there was nothing to hide there and told the DA she would and walked with him back to her office and unlocked the desktop. And allowed the uniformed policewomen to insert a one-terabyte thumb drive which almost filled up the thumb drive while they were waiting for it to download. A state police captain arrived to take charge of the proceedings, having been sent by the state attorney general and sent the sheriff's department and DA packing. When the thumb drive finished downloading, the captain pulled it out and handed it back to Elizabeth, saying the governor sent her regards. She put the thumb drive back into her desktop and erased it in case the county sheriff wanted it back. She then went to the lobby and told Linda that everything was ok and then left the clinic and went home to catch up on her sleep!

She closed her eyes, and a minute later, she awoke to her alarm clock ringing and got up and did her routine. Before she left, she called Charles and filled him in on what happened before heading off to work. She got her coffee and bear claw, and when she arrived at the clinic, she called Linda back to her office and went over what had happened and why and asked her about how she and the staff had reacted. She examined Linda's report on blood and was relieved to find that the AB Negative donors had returned, as well as most of the regulars. She then followed Linda back to the lobby and talked with the nurses, and explained any questions they had before sending them all home! As she returned to her office fifteen minutes before the dark bell rang, and she hurriedly brought the safe, laptop, and book back up and entered the report on today's business. She switched signs and put the lobby and hallways back into night mode and called up the 7 bottles of O negative, and, when the sun had set, released her guest from his room.

He returned the empty bottle of blood and thanked her profusely for letting him stay the day. He then took the seven bottles and quickly left. When he had gone, she released an antibacterial spray in the "day room," which completely sanitized it and closed off that section of the hallway. A state policeman sat outside the cul-de-sac and, by his presence, turned away several county sheriff deputies who had the idea of waiting to prey upon any vehicles that might leave the cul-de-sac. This service would continue until after the upcoming election when both the local DA and County Sheriff were destined to lose. When notified by the state policeman of what was happening, she called the state police captain and thanked him for the help. Back before the clinic was built, Richard had explained what he wanted to do to both the state and federal government, and all figured that by allowing the clinic, death and assaults by the vampires would drop dynamically, which it did. The "Weatherby Clinic" was just one of 41 similar clinics throughout America, each outside a major city in all but 11 states. The Weatherby Clinic wasn't the first but was third after clinics in New York City and Washington, D.C. Richard had heard about the clinic in New York City and modeled this clinic after that one. The one exception was that Detroit didn't have much of a subway system, so the cul-de-sac was needed, and they found one out in the suburbs.

As she looked out on the cul-de-sac, she noticed a bus pull into the parking lot and stopped by the side door. This was a leased bus coming in from Canada. Fortunately, it only had 24 vampires on board, as occasionally, it might have twice that many. Being Canadian, they were very polite and formed a line. Also, most had American money, so there was no trouble. The ones that didn't have gold Maple Leaf coins in either one oz, one-half oz, or one-quarter oz size. She had a program on her computer that gave her the exact amount and whatever change might be due, which she paid in US currency. Fortunately, she had only one ab negative customer, but still, he bought half of her supply. Thanks to the cooperation of her clients, they were all out her door in just under two hours! The customs people were hip, and the bus never had any trouble going back and forth across the border. In a year or two, she'd lose those clients as Canada was building its own dispensary, but so far, the closest Canadian one was in Ottawa.

When they had left, she looked at her current blood supply on the computer and wondered how long this current supply would last. She turned on the "Back in 5 minutes sign and took the money back to the vault and put it away, and then added the totals to both the laptop and the "book" and sent them all into the vault, still being a little paranoid after the police raid.

When she returned up front, she noticed the 5-minute sign was in a countdown, and she turned it off and buzzed them through. It was a pair of newbies who scanned the price menu sign up and down before ordering 6 O Negative bottles, two warm and four cold to go. She collected their $900 before giving them their two warm bottles and placing the other four bottles into a carrier, and sending it through the turn table. They asked about the hours we were open, and Elizabeth replied that it was from dusk until dawn six days a week, Monday through Saturday, although we were closed on the occasional Saturday, which would be announced several weeks in advance. Both here at the clinic or online at our site at: www.lifestreamlaboratories.com. She asked how they heard about the clinic, and they replied that Aristotle had mentioned us at a party in Grosse Pointe Woods, and everyone agreed that we must try it. They chatted for another 5 minutes until someone rang the doorbell, and she buzzed them through. It was the newbie couple from the other night who stopped and chatted with the couple leaving, who was apparently at the same party in Grosse Pointe Woods; what a small world, thought Elizabeth as they approached the counter. They ordered six bottles of O negative, two warm and four cold to go. And so, the evening went. After checking on the blood supply, she decided they needed to advertise the Weatherby Clinic on some of the local TV stations. A member of Charles's pack did such things, and she gave Charles a call and asked him to put her in touch with him to not only make the commercials but book the advertising too. The last time they had done this, they got a good response, and it had been months since she had an oversupply problem, even on O type. The Canadian AB Negative customer from tonight pointed out this need, and when dealing with vampires, it was better to be safe than sorry, as Richard found out!

As the sun rose, she set the clinic up for daytime activities and took Linda aside and explained her thoughts about advertising to her as Linda may be called upon to work as a nurse taking blood samples from the new donors before buying their blood. Last time they found a hippie tripping his brains out on LSD while trying to sell his blood and a couple of HIV patients. So, they needed one nurse to handle these would-be donors and make sure the blood supply was clean. They rearranged the lobby with another set of walls to keep the would-be donors and the donors apart. And since Linda had her master's in nursing, it fell to her to run the tests. With this settled, Elizabeth closed her office and went out to breakfast.

As she finished her breakfast and turned her coffee cup up and had a sip when she lowered it, Charles was sitting across from her. Charles said he had talked to David, and David would be calling her soon to discuss the proposition. Charles also thanked her for bringing the business their way! She replied, "Who else would I call? Who else could I trust? Anything I can send your way, I will!" He asked her what her plans were for tonight and tomorrow and if she would like to spend them with him. She had no plans and would enjoy his company, so it was settled. She would go home and change and then meet him at the castle, and perhaps David could join them when he had the campaign worked out, and they could finalize the deal.

She left him and went home, showered and changed

her clothes and packed a bag in case they went out on the town, and then drove over to his place. As the Caddy pulled into the driveway, the gates opened, and she drove up to the Castle to find Charles waiting there. He had her pull around to the back and park there, took her bag, and into the castle they went via the back door! The back door, like the front, was an armored affair opened by a key fob. Across from the door was an elevator but no staircases. The first and second floors were taken up by apartments where the pack lived. The third was not only a restaurant and, to one side, a kitchen and storage room. On the other side, a meeting room. They passed the fourth floor, and Elizabeth wondered what that looked like but didn't ask, with the fifth-floor door opening to Charles's apartment. Elizabeth hadn't noticed this door before, and when it closed, she knew why; as it descended, a floor section came up and took the place of the elevator.

Charles took her wrap and bag into the bedroom while Elizabeth looked at the paintings and things that covered the walls and wondered what it told her about werewolves. She realized she'd have to see what was on the walls of other pack members. His paintings were for the most part Baroque, Impressionism, Surrealism, and several stunning M.C. Escher prints with a couple of Man Ray statues! She certainly approved of his taste in art!

When Charles returned, he said he'd been talking to David, and David had some facts and figures for her perusal and was on the way up. The elevator doors opened, and David came out holding a laptop computer;

he took Charles aside and whispered something in his ear then they both glanced over at Elizabeth. They took seats around a small table, and David explained what he would do for the clinic, where he would place the ads and for how long, and what the total cost would be. He had whipped up three commercials and ran them explaining what each would do. Then talked about the cost for each station and what the total cost would be. When he was through, she was quite impressed with the commercials and his strategy and told him so. The only thing left for her was how to pay for them and when they would start. He gave her a sheet with his company's bank account information, the company's address and phone number, and his private phone number. As for when they would start, he wouldn't know until Monday but would get them going as soon as possible.

Elizabeth told him she would visit her bank on Monday and have the funds transferred to his account. When new donors came in, she would find out when and where they saw the commercials and what prompted them to act on them and let him know. David thanked her for the business and asked if he might ask a question about her business. She nodded her approval, knowing what the question might be. David asked, "Is it true your customers are vampires, and do you operate with the approval of the state and federal governments?" "Yes, David," Elizabeth said, "it's all true!" They spent the next 15 minutes making small talk until David got up, shook Elizabeth's hand, and left. Thank you, Charles. This is going to work out just fine, Elizabeth said as she moved next to Charles and gave him a kiss. What's on for tonight, Charles, anything planned? Elizabeth was hoping since she seldom had Saturday night off.

"I have two tickets for Tchaikovsky's Swan Lake at the Opera House if you'd care to go," said Charles.

"Yes, I would," said Elizabeth. "What a great idea, Charles," Elizabeth exclaimed. "I haven't been to the opera since Richard took me to see Verdi's Macbeth back when we were dating! You could tell it was in Detroit as in the scene where Banquo and Macbeth come upon the three witches, the weird sisters; you know: Double, double toil and trouble; Fire burn and cauldron bubble. Now the lights were low, so I could have missed a witch or two, but I counted 17 witches in all, not three; as you know, Detroit's a union town. I know I'll never see my favorite opera in Detroit, Béla Bartok's Duke Bluebeard's Castle."

"Why is that Elizabeth," Charles asked.

"Because it only has one set and two characters, Judith and Bluebeard," Elizabeth replied.

"C'est la vie," said Charles. "Now, let's get you to bed so that you can rest, and I'll get you up for dinner. Then it's off to the Opera House!" Elizabeth thought to protest but then realized that there would be plenty of time to make love when they got back, and then there was all day tomorrow too. So off to bed, she went.

Charles woke her up by kissing her all over, paying special attention to three spots in particular! After their lovemaking, they both got into the shower and afterward went down to the restaurant and had a delicious meal. Then it was off to the opera to a pair of second-row center seats; the front row was reserved for celebrities, cast members, family, and friends. Afterwards, they drank champagne before heading back to the castle for bedtime fun that lasted most of the night. They spent Sunday lounging around, and it was late Sunday night before Elizabeth left for home.

First thing Monday morning, Elizabeth went to her bank and sent David's company a wire for the total amount of the campaign. Then went back home and slept most of the day before arising just in time to head to work. She hadn't been to work for very long when David called with the start times for the various tv stations and affirmed they had received her payment. She took notes as she wanted to see that the commercials had run and run-on time, and if she couldn't watch them, then record them. She printed four copies of their schedule for her staff to watch just to make sure and get their opinions of them as well! When the fifteen minutes till sunset alarm had run, she handed out the schedules and asked if they could watch them and tell her their thoughts, then she sent them home.

As soon as they had left, she set the building on night mode and prepared to meet her clientele! She didn't have long to wait as apparently taking Saturday off made for anxious customers. A few minutes after sunset, about a dozen people crowded the lobby, and she was quite busy for a while filling their orders; when that crowd had left, she put on the "back in 5 minutes" sign and got the large double expresso that she had left in her office in a hurry to get the commercial schedule for her employees before they left. When she returned to the front, she noticed that the "back in 5 minutes" sign was in a countdown and buzzed the people through.

It was the Count who had come for his regular fix, i.e., a six-pack of AB Negative, one warm and five cold to go. This took up all of her AB Negative, so she hoped she'd get no more orders until the supply was replaced. Her clientele contained only three that could afford to buy AB Negative. She checked the computer and found that she had four bottles of AB Negative. She must have gotten them today. She hadn't glanced at Linda's report for today, so she went and got it from her office desk to see what it contained. The even better news was that her B-positive supply was back up to par. She really hoped the commercials would bring in the right donors. And so, the night went.

As the sun rose, she switched the clinic to daytime mode, welcomed her staff in, and went off to breakfast. It wasn't until she drained the coffee cup that Charles appeared out of thin air to tell her that he had to go out of town on business and wouldn't see her again until the day before the next full moon. He walked her out to her car, held her, kissed her for a minute, and said, "I Love You." Chills ran up and down her spine as Charles rarely spoke of his love for her. "I love you too," Elizabeth said as they kissed once more as he turned and walked away.

Two days later, the commercials started running on the local TV stations. The day after that, they began receiving appointments from new donors, mostly O and B donations but Halleluiah, two new AB Negative donors. By the end of the first week, they had a dozen new donors. At the beginning of the next week, the commercials on the History network began running, and they got another dozen donors from that account alone. Just in time too as the Canadians Bus came back, this time filled to the brim with 54 hungry customers. While the commercials were costly, the added profit they made more than covered their costs. She gave David a weekly report on the who and where, and when, which helped him refine their placements for future campaigns. Time went speeding by until it was the night before the day before the full moon. At the end of this shift, she would be back in her lover's arms again; she could hardly wait. She called Charles's number and got someone else who asked her who was calling; in the background, someone asked if it was the human girl, and another one said I thought he got rid of her, and the person who answered said Charles wasn't there but would soon be back and hung up.

As the sun rose, she got a call from Charles saying he was on his way and he'd meet her in her office in ten minutes or so. This was strange because Charles had never been to the clinic, much less to her office. She said she'd unlock the back door, and he should wait until she came out of the bathroom, and then they'd be off. She sent the laptop, "book," and safe to the floor and made herself into the bathroom to clean up before Charles arrived. She heard the backdoor open and close and took one more glance into the mirror before opening the door. She opened the door with her left hand and kept her right hand in the bathroom out of sight. There Charles sat in front of the desk on his hind quarters a very large and dangerous-looking werewolf. In a deep, dark voice, he said, "I'm sorry, Elizabeth, but the pack agreed that I must kill you as you already know too much; only I and David voted against it; I will make it quick; I'm sorry." As he got up and moved toward her, she pulled the 44-magnum with the silencer loaded with silver bullets out behind the wall and shot him. It didn't kill him, but it knocked him down. "I'm sorry that you drove me to do this, but the man who makes my wooden tip bullets made these silver tip bullets too," and then she shot him through the heart.

She then called the state police captain and told him what she'd done and where the nest of werewolves was, that they'd be locked in their cages and easy targets, and that they needed silver bullets. He assured her they already knew and had a good supply of silver bullets and would take care of the problem when the full moon rose. When the captain hung up, she called her cleaners and told the owner her problem, and he said they'd be right over. She wondered if she should keep the Bentley as it was miles above her Cadillac but decided to sell it for a pittance to a guy that would have it on a container ship and on the way to South America before dawn. The car was worth over $2 million. She wanted $10,000, but he offered her $25,000, and she took it!

THE GOD

He licked his lips; they were coming. He could hear the little boats coming down the river Styx. It had been nearly six months since he had tasted them, and his hunger was almost unbearable. Ah, it wouldn't be long now. He could hear their screams as they passed the minor devils and demons. They could do nothing to stop; it was too late for that. The river flowed only one way, and that was toward God; none could turn back once they started their journey. When they saw his magnificence, they would panic and try to escape, but none had, and none would. There was no escaping God.

Oh, they had tried. The females would scream and try and hide behind their mates. The males would remain calm, a false bravado that never lasted. Some would try and leap from the boats, but there was no escape. In the end, they would come to him and feed him well.

He flicked his tail and thought to himself about what these puny ones had done to deserve their fate. His master had created him for this task and this task alone. He had been spawned in the depths of Hell. He was known by many names in many places over the millennia. But most worshiped, sacrificed, and prayed to him as the great feathered serpent God Quetzalcoatl!

The fire marked their approach. It would be mere seconds until he quenched his hunger. Even now, he could see the first boat approach. Its passengers clung to each other in terror. Now they saw him. They screamed as they saw his huge jaws open to greet them. Boat after boat came to him, and he greeted and devoured them in a single bite. Ah, it was over; the screaming had stopped.

There had been ten boats. There had always been, and for all he knew, there always would be, ten. It mattered not, for they would come and feed him and feed him well. There was no escaping God.

Jeffrey Lowe and his wife Mary rode in such a boat with another couple whom they had just met. Mary had insisted that they come this way. It mattered little to Jeff, for it was her will, not his, that brought them on this journey. This would be their final stop. As they entered the cave, the sunlight disappeared, and they were alone in the dark. For the first time since the war, Jeff was becoming afraid. An Iraqi sand berm had collapsed on him while he was searching for it, and he had been trapped in it for almost a day. As he flashed back on the experience, he began to sweat. Since then, he had never liked being in dark places, and this place was pitch black. Up ahead, he could see a small point of light. As they approached it, a huge plume of fire sprang up in front of the boat, narrowly missing them. The couple in the back of the boat screamed, and Mary hugged him closer. When twin plumes of fire arose on both sides of the boat, Mary screamed, and for the first time since the war, Jeff was afraid of death, but wasn't that silly?

They rounded a bend in the river, and standing on the shore was what at first appeared to be a man. However, on closer inspection, they noticed it had a long, sinuous tail, cloven hoofs, and horns. As the boat drew nearer, it spoke.

"Welcome to your final reward; God awaits you," the demon said with a smile.

Jeff smiled at the thing, trying to hide his mounting fear. While holding Mary closer, he said, "Are they all as cute as you?"

The demon flicked his tail and drew his trident with a smile; "You will be lucky to fall on one that is as kind as I, for even if you escape them all, you will still meet the God." He then began to roar with laughter and swung the trident, barely missing and impaling them on its tines.

The little boat, with its four huddling passengers, moved on down the river toward only God knew what.

Now the demons and devils were all around them, reaching for them. Tails flicking, fangs extended, trying desperately to pull them from the boat. The noise was deafening, and the stench was horrible. Mary was nearly hysterical, and Jeff wasn't far from it either. Finally, they were beyond the reach of those on shore, and Jeff's fear somewhat subsided. He knew he was being silly but couldn't help himself in spite of this knowledge. Then suddenly, the boat rounded a bend in the river, and they came before the God, and they screamed.

He was huge with a massive set of jaws and row upon row of foot-long teeth. Bright blood-red eyes stared at them in a knowing way. They knew it had to be God, for who else could be so magnificent and so horrible at the same time? Fire erupted all around the boat, blocking any thought of escape, and the boat moved on into those massive jaws until everything turned scarlet...

With an explosion of sound and light, they were once again in the sunshine. The ride was over. Holding each other tight, Jeff and Mary left the amusement park.

A DEATH WISH

"Good afternoon students. Today's topic will be a murder mystery that I know you will enjoy solving. For if we, the people of Psittacidae, cannot understand why the Earthlings murder, how shall we be able to interact with them when we permit contact?"

"This is my favorite class, Earth Two. As a matter of introduction, my name is Yllop. Oh yes, we study you, Earthlings; we have for centuries. We pilot what you call 'Flying Saucers.' There is another such expression; how stupid of me to have forgotten it. Oh yes, you call it 'Swamp Gas.' We are about to watch a video that was made on a recent trip to Earth by one of our ships. It is titled, of all things, 'A Death Wish.' It seems to be about two Earthlings. One like us and"….

"Yllop, are you daydreaming again? See here, my fine young drib. Will you please pay attention?"

"Yes sir, sorry sir."

"Well, now, students, how shall we begin today's lecture? Since we cannot begin with a rekcarc break, we shall begin with the video."

"Hello, Earthlings, this is Yllop again. Before the video starts, I should mention this is not a movie. This was taken by one of our probes, and all that you will see actually happened. Ah, the video begins"……..

My dear God, here she comes again. Walter couldn't even believe it. He doubted if he could live another day with her. It wasn't that she was a bad person; it was just that she couldn't keep her mouth shut. Once she opened that huge cavern, she seldom shut it till bedtime. At least 95% of her time was spent talking to him. It was becoming so bad that he could hardly think. All Walter could ever see of her was her mouth twisted into that sickening smile and that voice. Dear Gods, that voice. She had decided that his vocabulary wasn't broad enough and had taken it upon herself to broaden it. Would he ever have any peace?

He never quite knew when the idea came to him. Once it did, the idea grew and grew until it was all-consuming. His race had the power, deep down inside, to make thoughts happen. He just had to get some peace. So, he began planning his "Death Wish."

"There you are. How is my little Walter doing today? Did you sleep well last night? Mommy fixed her little baby's breakfast. You look pale this morning. Is there anything wrong? Don't worry Mommy will call the doctor. Here drink some of this. You naughty boy, you shouldn't bite at Mother. Oh, it must be your fever. It's all right, dear, Mommy understands."

Walter wasn't sick, but he soon would be if she didn't shut her mouth. He couldn't take much more.

"Now you just sit right there, and Mother will go to the drug store and get you some medicine. It'll be a little while. Goodbye, precious."

At last, there was quiet. Quiet seemed to hang about the house. Maybe she wouldn't come back. Would he ever be that lucky?

Maybe her car would collide with another or hit a truck or a train. He didn't know how but one way or another, he had to get rid of her and for good.

He didn't remember the first time he had met her, although he couldn't possibly understand why he couldn't. That was a once-in-a-lifetime experience. How could he have forgotten? At least his memory spared him that. If only he didn't have to listen to her. She had always treated him nicely. He had a nice home and plenty of good food.

"Mother back. That stupid druggist said he didn't have any medicine for you. Perhaps if mommy makes a nice hot broth of chicken, it might make you better?"

"Shut up, you old hag!"

"Walter, how could you? Oh, it must be the fever. For a minute, I thought you might have meant it. You do love Mother, don't you? You are just Mother's little baby. Give Mother a kiss. Come on, Walter, give Mommy a big kiss!"

Walter took a big bite out of her nose!

"Walter, how could you! You've drawn blood! You might have broken my nose.... I'm sorry, I didn't mean to frighten you. Here, Mother is better. Look, it isn't bleeding too badly. I'll just go get a Band-Aid. I won't be a minute."

Walter was proud of himself. At long last, he had mustered up enough courage to strike back. If only he had enough courage to rid himself of her for good. He knew if he didn't do it pretty soon, she would drive him insane. Dear God, here she comes again.

"Mother back. Is my poor little Walter feeling any better? Why you're so weak you can barely stand up? Your eyes look so peaked. Mommy will make you your lunch. Oh, I know. I'll make that salad with all the passion fruit that you like. Now you just stay here, and Mommy will run to the store and buy some fresh fruit and vegetables for her baby. Walter, don't stick your tongue out like that. If I didn't know any better, I'd think you meant that to me. Now isn't that silly? Now you be a good boy while mama was gone."

Walter began his Death Wish again. If he only had the nerve to kill her himself. Even if he got up the nerve, he still wouldn't be able to do it himself. She was much too big and far too strong for him. Maybe if he used his hidden power and wished hard enough, the wish would come true. So, as she drove off, he intensified his thoughts.

How would he begin it? It would have to do its purpose without hurting anyone else. That would rule out a collision with another car or truck. Her car could get hit by a train, but someone else still might be hurt. All at once he had the idea, and with the idea came the wish. He didn't know anything about praying, but he thought a small prayer couldn't hurt. So he began...

He could see her in his mind's eye as she drove the big shiny car down the coastal highway. The highway ran along the ocean on a high cliff.

Almost three hundred feet to the ocean below, he had heard someone say. She is pressing the accelerator to the floor. The big car is beginning to pick up speed. Faster and faster until the needle stood at eighty; that should be fast enough. The sun is shining bright. There is a cool breeze coming in from the ocean. A bright shiny guard rail is on the left side of the car. On the other side, a gentle slope covered in grass. Up the road, a mile or so where the road goes into a curve, a truck carrying glass drops a small pane. The driver of the truck doesn't notice his loss and drives on.

"It's such a nice day, and the road is in good condition. I guess I could drive a little faster. After all, eighty isn't all that fast, and I haven't seen a policeman on this road in years. It is such a lovely day."

The left front tire runs over the broken windowpane. Suddenly she hears an explosion. The car careens out of control. The shiny new grill and bumper are crushed as they hit the steel rail. The guard rail is strong, but 4,000 pounds of metal traveling at 80 miles per hour snaps the rail in two. For a moment, the car seems to hang in the air. It sails like a leaf. Then suddenly, from out of nowhere, a jagged cliff arises, and the car explodes into a ball of flame. No longer the leaf but twisted fiery metal plummeting to the sea. It stays afloat for only a few seconds before swiftly sinking. High above the cliff, people gather to stand and watch helplessly. A police siren is heard, and then one from an ambulance, but they are already too late. Walter came out of his trance.

Walter hadn't felt this good in years. Had it actually happened? There was one fast way of finding out. He turned on the radio for the 12 o'clock local news. The clock showed 30 minutes until the hour when the time dragged on and on. He could hardly wait. He had to listen to an album side by a group called "Dead Politicians." He couldn't understand half of the words. Then there was a commercial about bad breath. She could have used some of that, he thought to himself. Would they never announce the news? Seconds took hours to pass, and minutes seem to take days! Then, at last, a man began to announce the news.

"…That wraps up the world news. Now turning to local news, this just in. A spectacular accident occurred this morning just north of the city. A car driven by Mrs. Walter R. Kellogg apparently crashed through a guard rail before plummeting three hundred feet into the sea. Witnesses said that Mrs. Kellogg lost control of the car when a front tire exploded."

Walter breathed a sigh of relief; his wish had come true.

"Fortunately, Mrs. Kellogg was thrown free of the car before it left the highway and suffered only minor injuries. In other news, students protested against…."

That was all Walter could take. He turned off the radio and sat down, and began to cry. Was he never to be rid of her? What was he to do now? It was all up to him. He knew he couldn't stand the sight of that mouth again. After all, it had been twelve years! Would there never be any peace? He knew if he didn't do it soon, he would lose his chance forever. He couldn't bear the thought of another twelve years. There was someone at the door. He could hear the voices of at least three people.

"You sure you're all right, lady?"

"Are you sure there isn't anything else we can do?"

"No, I'll be all right after I sit down for a while. Thank you very much; I'm perfectly all right now. Good-bye."

Heavenly Fathers, here she comes again!

"Walter darling, Mother is all right. She was just in a little accident. Nothing to worry about. Come sit on Mother's lap. Here I'll open the door for you. Come on; Mother wants to see you."

This was his last chance. Had he the courage? It was now or never. He flew at her with rage. A rage that had been building inside of him for twelve long years. Something snapped inside him. He found himself upon her. Hitting her with everything he had until she fell backward over a chair and snapped her neck on a marble-topped table with a sickening thud. She let out a gasp and then lay perfectly still.

It was over. Walter went back to his cage. No longer would she drive him insane. At last, there was peace in the house.

"Hello, Earthlings, this is Yllop again. Did you enjoy the video? It may be some time before I understand why Walter killed Mrs. Kellogg. In any event, I have the advantage over you. Remember when I tried to explain that this story took place between two Earthlings? One like us and…"

"Yllop, are you talking again?"

"Yes, sir. I was just trying to explain to the Earthlings about the video."

"Oh, excuse me, go right ahead."

"As I was saying about the two Earthlings before, my teacher interrupted me. One was like us, and one was human. You don't understand? We, the people of Psittacidae Four, are what you would call on Earth parrots. Who was the parrot in the video? Why, Walter of course. I'm sorry, but I must leave. The class has been dismissed, and I must get to my next class, Mars 101. Good-bye."

THE LADY AND THE DRAGON

Once upon a time, many years ago, in a far-off Kingdom, there lived a very beautiful Princess. However, our story doesn't concern her. In fact, the story concerns her very distant cousin and handmaiden to the Queen, Lady Grace.

Unfortunately, Grace was neither a lady nor, for that matter, a maiden. Having had given up her maidenhood many years before to a traveling troubadour, once she realized that her prince wasn't coming. Since then, there have been many a bold knight under her silken sheets, to the point where she'd lost count.

Also, in this Kingdom lived a very ancient and very wise Dragon named Mithridates. Mithridates had for years devoured knights and maidens alike and had become the scourge of the kingdom. But after a thousand years of this, he became bored by the same old scene. Capture a maiden or two and wait for the inevitable knight on horseback. Catch and eat the horse, battle the brave knight, and devour him, then. devour the fair maidens as well. This went on year after year, century after century until poor Mithridates was bored to tears. The once proud beast was beside himself in boredom. Not to mention that the effect of eating armor year after year was beginning to back up on his now delicate stomach. In a final desperate bid to end it all, he blew down the entrance to his cave, sealing himself in.

Time passed, and a thousand years came and went. And the memory of Mithridates faded from the kingdom. The once powerful beast first became a legend, then a myth and finally, was only invoked by mothers to scare their children into obeying them. "If you're not home by dark, Mithridates will get you and eat you up." In fact, Mithridates and his kind were now said to have never existed by the learned men of the kingdom. And who knows, they might have been right if the earthquake hadn't shaken the kingdom that dark day in May. For when it did, it opened Mithridates' cave and woke the sleeping dragon.

Mithridates opened one sleep-incrusted eye and looked around the cave from his position atop his hoard of gold. When he had inspected his lair and saw that all of his gold and jewels lay undisturbed, he closed his eye. As he was about to fall back asleep, aftershocks brought the entrance to the cave down. An explosion of light and dust broke upon the inner chamber where the great dragon lay. Mithridates was up now and with a centuries-clogged roar that sounded more like a cough than a roar, he made his way through the rubble and into the light.

After a thousand years of slumber, Mithridates found his muscles stiff, with a backache that went all the way down his spine to the tip of his tail. Not to mention the effects of not having gone to the bathroom in ten centuries! An hour or so later, Mithridates was feeling much better except for the overwhelming hunger in the pit of his stomach.

By now, even the knight's rusty armor had long since digested while he slept. Mithridates flexed his wing muscles, and the long sinuous wings unfolded from his back as he made ready to fly. He soon realized that he was exceedingly weak, and flying might not be a good idea. So as the sun set over the isle of Avalon, Mithridates made his way down the mountain from his lair and into a sheep pasture. By the time he staggered back to his cave, he had eaten 20 sheep and some infernal contraption that spoke to him in a strange but almost familiar language. It shot little arrows at him when he picked up a sheep and swallowed it whole. They sparked a bit as they harmlessly bounced off his scales, and as an afterthought, he turned and ate the thing and proceeded to slaughter most of the herd. When he had eaten his fill, he hiccupped up a knight's helmet that had been lodged in the hole in his throat from where he spits his dragon fire. When he did this, it caused him to sneeze and sneeze and sneeze again, setting fire to the meadow and most of the now screaming sheep. Feeling like a drunken sailor, Mithridates stumbled back to his bed and slept a fortnight.

Around Mithridates, the people of Westmorland County and, in particular, the village of Armory went about life, never suspecting what lay near the peak of Skyler's Mountain. From the top of the mountain on a clear day, you could see the Isle of Man. Most days, you could at least see the Irish Sea. There was much ado in the village today as the King's first cousin and lady-in-waiting to good Queen Elizabeth IV, the Lady Grace, was coming back to open her ancestral home in Kirk-wood Manor.

There was talk that her ladyship was bringing the good news about a new military spaceport for the county. Armory's chronically underemployed youth were becoming the scourge of European ultra-football matches. For the past two days, fleets of androids had been going over the manor from top to bottom in antici-pation of her ladyship's arrival. Nothing, of course, was ever officially announced about the travels of the royals, not since the Freemen terrorist strikes of 2081-2082.

When the smoke from that deadly six-month-long rampage ended, there weren't many blue bloods left. The ones that survived were a whole lot more concerned with the problems of their peasants than their forebears had been. And since the royals were for all intents and purposes powerless, the people made much of the remaining few. They were seen primarily as sources of entertainment and, of course, an ancient national tradition.

Lady Grace, the Duchess of Armory, dreaded this trip to her ancestral home. It was bad enough that she had to return to Earth from her block of flats in the

Lunar City of New London. She was, after all pushing 30, and she hated what Earth's gravity was doing to her body. Things were starting to droop! But James had called her back to earth to do her part in rebuilding England's economy. Since Scotland and Whales succeeded from the union, things had gone from good to bad almost overnight. Now James XI was spending almost a quarter of the crown's purse on the rebuilding of high-tech programs that might pull England out of debt and off the dole.

The big silver space liner fired its landing jets as it came in for a three-point landing, then taxied to the gate. Twin spaceways drove out from the building to meet the rocket. One for first-class passengers and the other for everybody else. Lady Grace was soon on board a nearby hopper for a flight to Kirkwood Manor. The hopper touched down in the courtyard, and Lady Grace was greeted by her private secretary Margaret who had flown on ahead.

Apparently, she needed to give a speech and symbolically turn a spade full of earth to signify the building of the spaceport. She'd be here for three days and then she could return to the moon. She spent the day going over the speech and a hundred other details with Margaret. After tossing and turning the night away on a mattress instead of her sleep beam, she arose late. After a late breakfast, she decides to skip another speech rehearsal and go horseback riding on the estate instead.

She mounts a chestnut mare, and with the aid of a fly Cam for protection, she heads out on a trail she hasn't been on since she was a girl. Up the side of Skyler's

Mountain, she rides to where she remembers a beautiful meadow. She'll ride there and beside the babbling brook, she'll have a snack of wine and cheese that Margaret thoughtfully packed before riding back to her responsibilities. Lady Grace wasn't prepared for what she found in the meadow.

The bank of clouds that had been sending forth a light mist suddenly opened up and the sun shone down on the valley of carnage. The once beautiful meadow was a charred wreck of its former self. The odor of burnt wood and wool lay over everything. The carcasses of a hundred sheep lay scattered about the meadow. Whatever had caused such destruction was gone, but she could feel its presence somewhere nearby, and so could her horse. As the horse started to whinny, she decided that she had seen enough and was about to turn and go when the horse reared up and threw her to the ground, and bolted toward her barn. She was getting back up and dusting herself off, silently cursing the horse when a huge shadow flew overhead, and a pair of claws reached out and grabbed the horse.

Mithridates had been sitting on a ledge watching the lady Grace for quite some time. He hadn't really planned to attack until he saw the horse bolt out from under her. Then his reflexes got the better of him, and he pushed off the ledge and made a beeline for the horse. As he tried to rise with the struggling animal, it became painfully clear to Mithridates that he still hadn't recovered from his 1000-year nap as he and the horse fell back to the ground with a crash. Lady Grace took one look at Mithridates and fainted dead away!

A long wet sensuous tongue brought her back to consciousness she found herself quite naked and looking into the jaws of a nightmare.

"Arrrrgh, my lady, fear thee not. I'll not eat thee, thissss day! Thy horse has ssated my hunger for now. Thou dost taste fair, but not as a virgin doth taste. What is thou husband'sss name?" Hissed Mithridates.

Lady Grace could not believe her eyes or ears. Was this all really happening? Surely, she must be dreaming, and Margaret would soon be awakening her. But she knew that what she saw was real. For every time she breathed, the rib she had cracked, from her fall off the horse sent a shooting pain down one side.

"Arrrrrrgh come ye now, my lady, I'll not harm thee, in fact, if thou hast gold or precioussss jewel, I'll make thee a bargain! Long have I ssslept and long has my preciousss hoard remained the same. I must at once make repairs to my hoard and seek yet more jewels and gold. So, tell me fair one, what is thy husband'sss name and rank? I must use this knowledge to make a bargain with him for thy ssswift release," spoke Mithridates.

"I am the Duchess of Armory, the Lady Grace. I am the lady-in-waiting for her Majesty Queen Elizabeth and cousin to the King. I have no husband, nor do I want one. This can't be happening; you cannot be real. You are but a nightmare that I will soon awaken from, be gone," said Grace.

"Haaassssst, thee have no husband? What manner of place is thisss? Hath common sense and moral'ssss flown away? Is this not still Avalon? Home of the Angle, Pict, Celt and SSSSaxonsssss? Did not mighty Rome once command these Isle'sss? Is thiss not the land of my youth? Tell me, my lady is thisss not so?"

"Well, dragon or hallucination or whatever you are, this is indeed England, called Avalon in legend. If you would live this day through, you will immediately give me back my clothes and be off with you before they come looking for me. I'm sure my flycam has captured all of this, and as I speak, there must be an army of soldiers on their way to rescue me."

Mithridates was a little taken back by this woman's tongue. Had she no respect for him or her position? He thought back through the long centuries for another such example, but I could find none. Finally, all he said was, "My name is Mithridates' and you're coming back to my cave to await your ransom." Saying this, he reached down and gently picked her up with his clawed hand. Holding her gently but firmly he unfurled his wings and rose slowly into the sky, and headed back to his lair.

Back at the estate, they knew something was wrong, and down in the village several hoppers were airborne and heading up the mountain to the meadow. The flycam had seen the horse throw Lady Grace and had focused on her as the Mithridates grabbed the horse and proceeded to crash to the ground directly on top of the flycam, which said nothing more with several tons of dragon on top. * So, all the android monitors saw Lady Grace fall off her horse, and then the view screen went black. They had been expecting to pick up her Ladyship and fly her back to her compound, so they were hardly prepared for the sight that awaited them. As grisly a scene as one found on any battlefield and absolutely no sign of her ladyship. Charred and rotting sheep flesh everywhere, the muzzle and reins of Lady Grace's horse, Lady Grace's clothing and boots were found, and a crushed flycam. Lady Constance de Coverlet, who piloted one of the hoppers, became violently sick and couldn't do much else for a while. *E=MC2

However, piloting the other hopper was Major Sir. T.K Chesterfield O.B.E.; late of the King's own Lunar Rangers, went right to work alerting the authorities and placing a viddy to his friend at the Palace, informing his majesty of the situation. He then proceeded to scour the countryside looking for clues and had several marked off when Chief Constable Thackery arrived.

"Good morning, Major," said the Constable. "What's all this, then?"

"Very peculiar, Constable Thackery. Just let me point out a few oddities to you. I've touched nothing but had these spots marked out on the hopper's viewer to point out a few clues. Oh, Lady Constance did disturb one spot with the remains of her breakfast but other than that, it's as we found it. For example, this is all that is left of Lady Grace's horse, about half of her nose," said the Major. He touched the screen and it showed a close-up of the mare's remains. "This is a pile of Lady Grace's clothes, Constable. Here, here, and here something ate and burned a flock of sheep," and various piles of bones and rotting wool passed the screen. "That's a crushed flycam in case you couldn't tell what it was. Oh, and the strangest thing of all. Now there aren't many of these, as I supposed the ground is too rocky, but look at these tracks. Have you ever seen anything like them? Three clawed talons like birds or dinosaurs but another clawed toe facing the other way, kind of like an opposable thumb!"

"Well, thank you, Major. You've given me a lot to think about; if we need you, we'll be in touch," said the Chief Constable, dismissing the Major out of hand. Then looking down the mountain, he saw the crime-lab hopper making its way up. Dinosaurs indeed! He'd soon get to the bottom of this! The crown was probably already watching over his shoulder, and he wasn't about to be found wanting in any way!

Lady Grace realized she was sleeping, but it felt so good. She was warm and content for the moment, and she reached out and wrapped her arms around a taloned finger. Ah, so nice and comfy. AAAAAAAAAAAAaa she screamed as she opened her eyes with a start to the looks of a much-bemused Mithridates.

"Hasst my Lady had her fill of sssleep yet? We must talk of the thing to come. To ransom thee; I will thisss day begin! Now what, my Lady, shall be thy price? I will seek a full hundred head of cattle. Plus, thy weight in gold and precious gems and five full barrels of wooly beer. This, to me, they will deliver within the fortnight or else!"

"Or else what, wyrm?" Asked Lady Grace.

"Or else I will be forced to eat you up and find another fair damsel, milady," said Mithridates with an evil grin that sent a chill to the very core of Lady Grace.

"Now, where is my parchment and quill?"

Constable Sgt. Tuttle re-read the evidence and

conclusions coming out of the crime-lab. No, the Chief Constable was not going to be pleased. No, not one bit, but there it was. He'd checked the machine over from top to bottom, and it was working perfectly. He'd submitted everything they knew about the case plus all of the crime-lab's findings from all of its sensors three times, and the results were exactly the same. A fire-breathing nightmare from fairy stories was alive and on the loose in 22nd-century England.

"Is that report finished, sergeant? The Minister for Public Safety has been on the viddy all morning. Let's hope this analysis clears things up. I would hate to post the Major's conclusions to the crown."

The sergeant said nothing but handed the viewer to the Chief Constable and waited for the explosion, he didn't have long to wait.

"Yesss, that ssshould do. Aaarrrrg, where didssst I place that sssealing wax and my signet? It could hardly be considered a true writ without my seal! Aaarrrrgh tisssss here aha! I shall roll the parchment and seal it thusss and thence deliver to your ladyship'ssss manor at the stroke of midnight! Now come talk to me, my lady of this 22nd century!"

"Constable Tuttle, what does this mean?" Said Chief Constable Thackery.

"Well, sir, according to the evidence and ancient evidence through the Royal data bank, what we have here is a Dragon who has kidnapped Lady Grace and will probably offer her for ransom. Yes, I know how that sounds, sir, and I wish I could say it's not so, but that is the conclusion of the crime labs computers." If you noticed I triple-checked them and ran a complete diagnostic on the main frame. That's the crime-labs report, and it's sticking to it.

Of course, the Chief Constable didn't believe it and called for another crime lab. At about midnight, the new machine was making the same report to a highly agitated Chief Constable Thackery. Mithridates left the sheepskin at the front door of Kirkwood Manor quietly returned to his lair without setting off a single alarm. Ten minutes later, a passing security bot found it, and all hell broke loose. Although Mithridates had managed to avoid the cameras; his shadow hadn't. It was there on two cameras for the entire world to see. And deny it all he liked the Chief Constable finally, he was forced to see the light in the shadow and his crime-lab reports.

The sheepskin was poured over first by the security bots and then by the Chief Constable and then the crime lab. Although a bit hard to read the Middle English soon gave up all its words and intent to the computers. It was a shaky, nervous Chief Constable Thackery who stood at attention and gave his report over the viddie to James XI. The King didn't laugh or even question the Constable, which was good, because Thackery was ready to faint at the drop of a hat as it was. He just took everything that Thackery said as truth and thanked the Constable for his report, concluding that he was on his way to intercede for his cousin in any negotiations.

Of course, there was nothing to negotiate. Either Mithridates got his beer, gold and cattle or the royal family was going to be one member short. It was only his greed for more gold that had kept Grace from becoming a snack, to begin with. Mithridates hiccupped and spit four steel horseshoes out and eyed them as they rolled around. Horses with metal feet, what would they think of next?

The British defense network was about to show Mithridates just that in a low flying hopper that had discovered Mithridates cave and was shining its spot-lights inside. Fortunately for the hopper pilot and Lady Grace, they didn't reach the inner lair. For Mithridates was a dragon of his word. Had he not captured the Lady Fair and square? He had not harmed her and never would if the ransom was paid. If, however, he found that the humans didn't stick to his agreement; he would indeed eat the lady and whoever he found to be lacking in the honesty department. There was nothing personal about it, just fair was fair. Now all that was to do was to wait and see if the humans complied? He spent the next two weeks talking to Grace about this new world he had been reborn in. Seems quite a bit has changed in the last ten centuries!

He fed the Lady Grace wine, cheese, and bread he was able to find in a nearby cottage. The owners were away when he called, which was just as well as Mithridates was starting to get hungry again. The horse and the sheep were starting to wear off, and he knew it would be the cattle or Lady Grace if the moon arose on an empty field.

The time had arrived, and he grabbed the Lady Grace again and looked hard and long at what lay below him, he turned to her and spoke. "Methinksss the King is fond of thee milady? I see a herd of cattle; five bright barrels of what must be beer and a pile of gold. I will set thee free. However, if this proves to be a trick, I will hunt thee down and devour thee, this I promise though you run to the ends of the earth!" The great dragon leapt into space with the Lady Grace held gently in one hand. He flew her to her manor house and landing just outside the wall, put her down gently and then gave her one last lick from her head to her toes, perhaps to remind himself of her taste and smell. Then, in an instant, he was gone, and Grace stumbled toward the gates and safety.

Not knowing what was going to happen, the King had delivered exactly what Mithridates had demanded, plus a little something else, a tracker. Mithridates scooped up a steer and swallowed it whole, and then grabbed another. He took his time and chewed this one savoring the taste and aroma. It took him a minute to figure out how to open the barrel, but then in quick succession, he opened and drank three of the barrels and turned his attention to the gold.

While this was happening, Lady Grace was found and reunited with her cousin and some clothes. She had just begun to feel secure again when the King told her about the tracking device. "Oh No," she screamed. "You mustn't do anything like that. If you don't keep your bargain, he will eat me. You can't use that; he's very smart, very clever, no, you can't do this!" Even though the King assured her that the armed forces were standing by to attack the King's command; she would have none of it. Stopping only to get dressed, she ran out to her hopper and set it a course to the London Spaceport. Just as her rocket was taking off, all hell broke loose on Skyler's Mountain.

As soon as the gold was moved, the King launched his attack. Wave after wave of fighters and hoppers made Mithridates cave a living hell. When the bombing stopped, and the top half of the mountain was gone. Shock troops found the lair, and its huge hoard of gold and gems. Enough, perhaps, to make Britain great again.

Search though they did; they never found the dragon's body. Eventually, it was said to have been destroyed in the bombing, although there was never a trace of the huge Dragon was found.

It was a little over a year later that a knock came on the window of Lady Grace New London lunar flat. A neat trick considering that window was 600 feet from the ground, and there was no air or air pressure on the outside. She knew who it was and tried to make a dash for the doorway when that window suddenly collapsed outward and she was sucked out of her flat and into the waiting jaws of Mithridates, chomp!

When would these mortals ever learn to play fair? Did she think that running to the moon would save her. Didn't she know that Mithridates and his kind were space-faring people. How did they think Mithridates came to be? He flipped his wings and rose high above the moon. He thought it might be nice to visit his parents again, and so he set off toward Betelgeuse and home!

HE NEVER CAME BACK

"Shore gonna be a fine night for fox hunting, Zeke."

"Yep, I reckon it will, Jody."

"Has ya ever seen such a bright moon?"

"Can't say that I have, Jody."

"Listen to yonder; sounds like old Jeff has started one."

"Yep, I can hear Lady joining him. Did you bring your bag, Jody?"

"Shore did. I rolled up six fat boys."

"Well, fire one up."

"Here ya go; what the hell is that over there, Zeke?"

"I don't know, Jody, but let's get the hell out of here…!"

Time: The present.

Place: The mountains of southeastern Kentucky.

"Where's that report on that double murder, down in Pike County, Johnson?"

"I'm just finishing it up right now, Captain Tracy. Strangest thing I've ever seen."

"Did the coroner make his report yet?"

"No sir, we haven't found enough of them to fill an envelope; parts of them were found in Virginia. The only reason we know who they are is the DNA tests that came back this morning. Since the remains were found in two states, the boss has called in the FBI. They've sent an agent down, and he's waiting in your office, Captain."

"I'll go talk with him now. You keep on it, Sergeant!"

"Yes, sir."

"Captain Tracy? I'm Special Agent Brown, James Brown, FBI."

"Glad to meet you, Agent Brown. How can I be of service?"

"Well, Captain, I've read the report, and I find it hard to believe. Is there anything you can add to it?"

"Just that we know who they were and what they were doing there. Their names were Jonah Grey and Ezekiel Williams. They were farm boys from Pike County and were out running foxes with their hounds."

"Did you find any more of them?"

"We've found traces of them over 400 acres extending into Virginia. There is nothing left. Whatever hit them is something new. No one's ever seen anything like it."

"Well, I'm going to take a drive down there and see for myself. If I find out anything, I'll be in touch. Good day to you, Captain."

"Good Luck to you, Agent Brown, and good hunting."

When I left Lexington that hot August afternoon and pointed the car toward Pike County, I had no idea what I was looking for. The report had made no sense. Two good ole boys murdered, and their remains spread over two states. Short of atomics, what in the hell could they do that? Well, I had a couple of hours to mull it over as I drove toward eastern Kentucky.

The flat farmlands fell away as I approached the mountains and my destination. This was coal country, and the land was scarred from open pit strip mines. As I left the freeway and headed into the backwoods, I found myself surrounded by giant coal trucks, a very uncomfortable feeling. The sun was beginning to set as I reached my destination, the sprawling metropolis of Little Creek, Kentucky, with a population of 342. Most of that staggering figure lived up in the hills.

The only hotel in town was the two rooms over the building that served as a post office, bar and grill, gas station, and morgue. These rooms were normally used when a trucker would misjudge a curve, and he and his rig would sail off into Limbo. On Saturday nights, this was the noisiest morgue in town. The only other building in town was a Protestant church, which by the looks of it, hadn't seen any services in fifty years.

However, even this didn't keep me from my duties. My "date" didn't seem to be thrilled by the two late truck drivers, stacked in the bed beside us. I had checked in, and the girl behind the desk had knocked on my door moments later, carrying towels and a smile. The next thing I knew, she was all over me, and the rest is history. My two truck-driving friends slept late; at least they hadn't arisen when I awoke, around noon. Strange, I thought, as I normally get up around 7 a.m. I quickly washed up in the bowl and pitcher provided and made my way downstairs.

There, waiting for me at the bottom of the stairs, was the proprietor of this little complex, Mr. Benjamin Baldwell. He kindly opened the bar for me, and after a couple of eye-openers, he introduced himself and insisted I call him "Uncle Ben." I, however, addressed him as Mr. Baldwell as he didn't look a thing like my Uncle Ben.

He introduced me to his daughter Cindy Lou, whom I had met the night before but never got her name. He assured me that she was 18, a high school graduate, and quite a good cook and was going to make someone a fine wife.

He also said she knew where the boys had been the other night and suggested she show me around. I took him up on that offer and left with my guide and native interpreter, good ole Cindy Lou. As we left the building and made our way to the car, Uncle Ben walked out after us and smiled and waved goodbye as we pulled away.

Our first stop was at the victims' farms, where I met the grieving parents and siblings. They had nothing to add to the Kentucky State Police reports, so I had Cindy Lou direct me to the area where the bodies were found. After a two-mile hike back into the woods, we came upon the murder scene. It was a complete mess. Everything in sight had a slight red tint to it. It was like the bodies had been placed in a woodchipper again and again, and what was left was sprayed over everything. There was a sweet smell to the place that couldn't be explained. After searching the area, we made our way back to the car, where good ole Cindy Lou turned to me with that space cadet glow in her eyes. After a time... or a few times, I returned to the car with that glow in my eyes too.

Cindy Lou turned to me and said, "Folks around here say it was the 'Swamp Monster' that got 'em."

"The Swamp Monster?"

"Sure, daddy says that the monster has been taking folks since the end of the war."

"Which war was that?" I queried. "Afghanistan, Iraq, Vietnam, Korea, World War Two?"

"The War of Northern Aggression," she replied.

So, what we have here is an ALF, running loose for well over a hundred and fifty years? I knew the people around here hadn't trusted the Federal Government since the whiskey tax of the 1790s, and who could blame them? I also realized that most government employees were there because they couldn't make it in the real world, except of course, for me. However, I wasn't going to fall for this old wife's tale.

"Well then, where does this monster live," I asked.

"In a cave over by Red Ridge. If you like, I can show you where, but I'm not going in," she replied.

"No problem, you can wait in the car while I go check it out," I said.

She gave me the directions, and we headed out toward the monster's lair. It was about a half-hour drive down two-track roads over the hills and across the valley to the next ridge. When we arrived at the bottom of the ridge, she pointed out the cave and, with the help of a pair of binoculars, I finally found it. I left good ole Cindy Lou in the car, and after checking the clip and laser sights on my 10 mm., I started the climb up the mountain.

"You be careful, James," she cried as I watched her lock the doors on the Navigator.

I set out in the general direction of the cave, and in about 45 minutes, I finally found it. It was dark, deep, and cool as I entered, and again, I noticed the same sweet smell. I had the distinct impression that I was being watched, and I drew my service pistol and nervously flicked the laser sight on. The cave itself, though wide at the mouth, soon narrowed to almost nothing, and then ended abruptly. Well, if the monster lived here, it wasn't at home, nor was there any sign other than the sweet odor that it had ever been here. After a thorough search of the cave, I began to make my way back down the mountain when I heard a blood-curdling scream.

I could see the car through the treetops, and as I made my way down, I began to see a change come over it. Its bright shiny white paint job had now turned to a bright red. I didn't like the feeling of Deja Vu I was beginning to have, either.

When I, at last, broke through the bushes and came upon the car, my worst fears came true. All that was left of Cindy Lou was sprayed around the entire area. Although I searched the entire area around the car, there were no clues, evidence, or even a track in the soft earth. Whatever had attacked Cindy Lou had managed to do it without even opening the door to the car, as it was still locked. However, the inside of the car was completely clean, as if she had left the car when she was attacked. As Alice in Wonderland once stated, "Curiouser and Curiouser!"

After an ever-widening search around the area, I finally gave up and headed back to Little Creek. On the way back to town, I was hit by a thunderstorm, and by the time I arrived, the Lincoln was back to its pristine white condition. As I arrived back at the hotel, I was greeted by "Uncle Ben," who was sitting on the porch, rocking in a rocking chair.

"Howdy there, boy; where's my daughter?" He asked.

"Oh, I dropped her off down the road; she said she wanted to visit some friends," I lied.

"Well then, come up here and sit a spell and let's jaw fur a while," he replied.

As I walked to the porch and took a seat, he asked me if I'd found the swamp monster. I told him no and asked him to tell me what he knew about it.

"I reckon the critter has been roaming these hills for over 150 years. My great-grandpappy's pap told him that the monster came one night in 1864 when them 'Damn Yankees were driving our boys back into Virginia. There was a big explosion up on Red Ridge and when the sun came up, the Yankees were gone; the entire ridge had turned red, and all the trees for a square mile had been knocked down. Since then, folks have stayed away from up there," he said.

"Is that all there is to the story?" I asked. "Does anyone know any more about it?"

"Well, there's Grandpa Jones; he's 114 years old, and

if anybody knows more about it than me, it would be him. He lives with his great-granddaughter over in Piney Hollor. Let me get my other daughter, Candy Jane, and she can take you there if you have a mind to," he said as he got up and shuffled back inside.

He soon reappeared with his other daughter, good ole Candy Jane. She was either an identical twin of Cindy Lou, or else Uncle Ben was playing head games with me. Either way, I was beginning to smell a rat, and it smelled just like Uncle Ben.

"Hi, I'm Candy Jane," she said as she shook my hand, "You must be Agent Brown? My daddy has told me all about you. Pleased to meet you."

"Please, call me James. Your daddy tells me you can direct me to Grandpa Jones's house," I asked.

"Why sure I can, it's just down the road a piece, over in Piney Hollor. My, you have a purdey car," she said with a big grin.

"It's a government perk," I said as I turned the Lincoln around and headed off to Piney Hollor, er, Hollow.

"You take the left fork up ahead and then look for an old barn with a Mail Pouch sign painted on it. You turn right there, and Grandpa Jones's farm is the first one on the left," she said.

As I followed Candy Jane's instructions, I watched her out of the corner of my eye and had to laugh to myself as she explored the car. It was like watching a child at Christmas. It was all so new and exciting to her. I almost missed our turn because the barn in question had fallen in upon itself and was now just a pile of rotting lumber. As I turned off the paved road and down into the hollow, I began to smell that sweet odor again, and when we turned into the Jones farm, I was met by a familiar sight.

The house, barn, and outbuildings were covered by red slime, a fact that wasn't lost on Candy Jane.

"Look, James, the Swamp Monster got 'em," she noted.

I pulled the Lincoln up to the house and quickly got out, drawing my gun.

"Stay in the car," I said as I made my way into the house.

"Uh uh," she replied as she quickly joined me on the porch. "I ain't staying in the car with the monster about."

"Well then, stay close to me but keep out of my line of sight," I told her as I took her hand in my left hand while I flipped the safety off the automatic with my right.

I cautiously opened the front door and entered the house. The inside was much like the outside, covered floor to ceiling in a slick red gore. We searched the house from top to bottom, but there was no one at home. There was a dinner set out on the table, and the food was still warm. Whatever happened here had just happened. I could feel the hairs on the nape of my neck standing on end. As we left the house, a shot rang out and tore a chunk out of the door as I dropped to a crouch and fired off a couple of rounds in the general direction of the sniper. Another shot rang out and dropped Candy Jane at my feet. A neat hole through the center of her forehead stared back at me, giving her the appearance of having three eyes.

I dove off the porch, firing the rest of the clip as I scrambled for cover. I crawled under the porch and slipped another clip into the gun while I scanned the area, looking for a target. It suddenly came to me that it was dead quiet. There was absolutely no sound of any kind except for the beating of my heart. Not a bird, insect, or even the trembling of a leaf. An absolute hush had descended on Piney Hollow. The Lincoln was parked about ten yards away, and if I could get to it, I could call for backup on the cell phone. I waited about ten minutes, and as there was no more fire from the sniper, I began to crawl to the car. I made the car and got in, and "fired that mother up." As I looked back at the porch I noticed that Candy Jane was gone!

Well, what the hell. As I headed out the driveway and onto the road, the back and front windshields exploded as another round whistled past my ear. I had been told the car was equipped with bulletproof glass. I didn't give it another thought as I found the paved road and turned onto it, and headed back to town. When I had covered about a mile, I pulled out the cell phone to call Washington, but for some reason, the phone wasn't working. I'd have to find a pay phone somewhere. Although I took the same route back, I couldn't find Little Creek. After a couple of hours' search, I found myself fast approaching the city of London, Kentucky. How in the hell had I gotten here? I was at least a hundred miles away from Little Creek. I pulled into a Ford dealership to use the phone and see about repairs to the car. I left the car in the lot and made my way to the office.

After seeing about the car, I asked to use the phone and placed a call to my boss in Washington. When I reached him, I gave my report, knowing full well the kind of reception it was going to meet. I wasn't disappointed by his reaction.

"Brown are you drunk? Have you been smoking those funny cigarettes and watching the X-Files again? I can't give the Director your report if I want to keep my job. What in the hell is going on out there? You better put that Kentucky Bourbon down if you want to keep your job," he kindly spoke.

"Sir, I know it's hard to believe, but every word is true," I replied.

"Well, where are you now?" He asked.

"I'm at a Ford dealership in London waiting to get the car windshields fixed."

"You just stay there. I'm sending out a team to join you. They'll be there in two hours. Don't move a muscle. Do you understand me, Brown?"

"Yes, sir, not to move a muscle," I replied."

Good, it will give you time to sober up. Goodbye," he said as he hung up.

Well, there goes the raise I had been expecting. I didn't have time to muse about this turn of events as I was approached by the head mechanic, Floyd, who had some disturbing news for me.

"Excuse me, sir, are you Agent Brown?"

"Yes, I am. What can I do for you, uh, Floyd?"

"Well, sir, it's about your car," he said.

"What about it?"

"Well, sir, we couldn't find anything wrong with it. There's not a scratch on it."

Well, that was par for the course. Maybe the chief was right. Maybe I was losing my mind. No. I knew I wasn't hallucinating. There was something going on in Little Creek and I was going to get to the bottom of it before the other agents hit town.

"Uh, Floyd, can you give me directions back to Little Creek?"

"Sorry, Agent Brown, I've never heard of it, but let me ask the boys," he replied.

He left but soon returned with an elderly gentleman in tow.

"Mr. Campbell here says he knows how to get there. Go ahead, Bill, tell this feller how to get to Little Creek," Floyd said.

"Well, sir, if I recollect, it's just a little south of Pikeville over by the Virginia line but why would you want to go there? No bodies lived there since the end of the War Between the States. Taint nothin' there but a ghost town," he said.

Oh joy, I was afraid of something like that. He gave me directions, and I left them to talk about the crazy G-man and headed off in the direction he gave me. The car's wind screens were intact, and when I saw that, I felt the hairs stand up on my neck again. I had an hour and a half to think about what had transpired in the last couple of days, and something that JFK was said to say stuck in my mind, "Don't get mad, get even!" Well, payback was going to be Hell. This was no longer a job but had gotten really personal, and I was going to get to the bottom of this come hell or high water.

When I crossed the last ridge, I could see Little Creek in the valley below and what the old man said seemed to be true. Where the hotel had been was a pile of rubble across the street, the church was in the same condition. Still, I drove on down into the valley. As I drove over the last rise and into town, I found myself confronted with the town as I had left it this morning. There on the porch sat Uncle Ben rocking in his chair, and next to him sat a very much alive Candy Jane.

"Well, that's that. I just gave up smoking and drinking; I thought as I pulled up in front of the general store, gas station, bar and grill, morgue, and hotel. I see you made it back, Agent Brown. They fixed up your car as good as new," said Uncle Ben with a big ear-to-ear grin.

"Would someone like to let me in on the joke," I said.

"What joke is that?" Replied Uncle Ben.

"Oh, and by the way, Candy Jane, how are you feeling? What happened to that beauty mark you had on your forehead, honey child? You're much prettier without it," I said.

"Why, James, whatever do you mean?" Candy Jane replied.

I was just about to get really pissed off when we were joined by Cindy Lou, carrying a pitcher of iced tea and some glasses. As she placed the pitcher and glasses down, she pulled a third arm out and began to comb her hair with it. As the world started to spin around, the last thing I remember is Uncle Ben slapping his sides and roaring with laughter.

When I awoke, the town had turned back into rubble. Over on my left, I can see what appears to be a spacecraft. It's hard to say, as the images around it are all slippery. It seems to be fading in and out of my vision. Cindy Lou and Candy Jane are waving to me. I think I'll go see what they want. I'm leaving this digital report for you and turning on the emergency beeper. I hope to finish it up before you arrive.

"And that's the entire report, Inspector?"

"I'm afraid it is, chief. That's all we found, sir."

"Now, what in the hell can I tell the Director? A tale of spaceships and three-armed girls. He'll have my guts for garters. Did you drag me down here to see a burnt spot in the grass? Well, maybe, if I bring the Director Agent Brown's head on a silver platter, I can keep my job. And where in the hell is Brown anyway, Inspector?"

"Brown, sir? He never came back!"

WINKY TINKY'S CHRISTMAS ADVENTURE

With his hands on his hips, Santa stood looking into the mirror. Ho Ho Ho Ho, he laughed with glee as he turned to Mrs. Kringle; his long- suffering wife, to show her the results of the three weeks of Viagra. She mused to herself, "Where was that a thousand years ago when I needed it?" There would be no living with him as long as he kept taking those darn pills, she thought, as she finished knitting another pair of socks for the Elves. As Santa turned to admire himself again in the mirror, Mrs. Kringle put her knitting away and left the bedroom, and made her way downstairs to the Toyshop.

She walked past benches laden with half-assembled toys and long rows of Elves busily constructing them until she came to where the chief, Elf Bimbo, stood chewing out the littlest of all the Elves, Winky Tinky.

"Now see here, Mr. Tinky, I've told you at least a

hundred times today to put tab B into slot A. If it wasn't for Christmas being only two weeks away, I'd toss your sorry as_... Oh, good morning Mrs. Kringle," Bimbo said, pulling up short.

"Here are your socks Bimbo," Mrs. Kringle said. "Try to keep them on your feet this time and off of your pe___..."

Just then, a whistle blew, marking the lunch hour and ending the conversation as all the Elves began to rush out of the room. Randy, little buggers, Mrs. Kringle thought to herself as she smiled and slowly shook her head.

Winky Tinky loved 'Lunch Hour,' as it allowed him to visit the reindeer. He merrily skipped out the door of the workshop and across the compound past groups of Elves waiting in line outside the kitchens, past the chemical laboratories where white-coated Elves were putting down their beakers and untying their aprons from their work, making the "magic dust" that allowed the reindeer to fly. Until he came at last to the big red barn where the reindeer lived, he struggled with a bale of hay until he could climb upon it and pull the latch back that unlocked the big barn doors. He leaped from the bale and scampered through the doors and into the barn.

The smells of hay, barley, oats, and reindeer droppings permeated the barn and made Winky Tinky smile. There they all were in their own special stalls...

He watched Dancer and Prancer nuzzling one another over the bars of their stalls. Dancer had recently come out of the closet, much to the delight of that old queen Prancer. Next came Dasher, who was busy running in circles in his stall, the result of overdosing on 'speed' again. In the next stall was Vixen, the only female reindeer in the group, who was busy counting some money and rubbing her behind from Blitzen, who had just returned to his stall from visiting Vixen. Just beyond Blitzen's stall was a stall surrounded by barbed wire and a reindeer that was tied up to a hand cart with a hockey mask over his muzzle. When Winky came to the stall, he moved out into the center of the barn; no need to give Donner the cannibal a chance at him. He stayed out away from the stalls as he passed Cupid, who would nail anything that walked. Cupid whistled at him as he walked by and batted his eyelashes. Next came Comet, the genius of the group, who was busy working on a j.a.t.o (jet-assisted take-off) system. Till, at last, he came to Rudolph's stall.

Rudolph, beautiful Rudolph. Winky's little heart skipped a beat as he gazed into Rudolph's golden eyes. Here was love; here was everything Winky had ever wanted. If only Rudolph felt the same way. But alas, Rudolph didn't share Winky's feelings. In fact, Rudolph could be downright hostile to the littlest Elf. Had, in fact, tried on several occasions to gore Winky with his antlers. He had even tried to kick Winky with his hooves. Rudolph's action did nothing to sway Winky's longings; in fact, it had just the opposite effect. Winky yearned even more for Rudolph! Winky stood there with a silly grin on his face as he reached into his jacket and pulled forth a bunch of asparagus.

Asparagus was the one gift Rudolph couldn't refuse. Asparagus was what Santa used to feed the reindeer after their Christmas flights as a reward. The Reindeer loved Asparagus and would do practically anything to get some. Rudolph stopped his hostility toward Winky and began to wag his little tail and prance around the stall. Winky held out a single stalk toward Rudolph, which the reindeer quickly grabbed and wolfed down, then looked up, hoping for more. Winky shook his head no and waited expectedly for Rudolph to turn around. Rudolph meekly turned around and offered Winky what he wanted. Winky quickly climbed up the bars and then leaped on Rudolph's back. He threw the stalks of Asparagus onto the ground, and as Rudolph grazed, Winky started to remove his pants.

Just as he was beginning to mount the reindeer, Santa came and grabbed Winky by his collar and pulled him out of the stall. "I thought I told you to stay out of the barn Winky," said Santa. He put the little Elf down and, with a smack on his behind, sent Winky out of the barn. Randy, little beggars thought Santa. Santa then turned and popped a couple more Viagra's as he walked down to Vixen's stall, where he pulled out a bunch of Asparagus. A few moments later, reindeer screams and Santa's Ho Ho Hos rang out all across the compound.

Winky was crestfallen; he hung his head low and fought back the tears as he left the barn. Rumple Tweezer: the shop steward turned to Bimbo, sadly shaking his head, and said, "Poor little Winky, there will be no consoling him again."

"Yeah," said Bimbo. "I wish Santa would let him score; I might be able to get some work out of him. Poor lovesick little Elf."

Winky knew that the other Elves were talking about him behind his back, but he didn't care. Nothing mattered to him anymore, nothing but Rudolph. Those deep golden eyes, the way he pranced, the sinuous curve of his antlers, his cute little tail, his shiny black hooves, and that shiny red nose, ohhhh, that little red nose. He couldn't eat, couldn't sleep, and couldn't keep his mind on anything but beautiful Rudolph.

His every attempt to see his beloved Rudolph alone seemed to be blocked. No matter what he tried, he seemed to be doomed by kismet to be kept ever apart. Fate seemed to be against him, yet his desires drove him on! Once, he even snuck out of the Elves' bunkhouse for a midnight tryst and got into Donner's stall by mistake. Winky was still having a series of nightmares about it. Would fate never smile upon poor Winky?

As the days and nights ticked off until Christmas, the Elves were kept very busy. Long did they labor at the almost impossible task of assembling the toys and packing them in Santa's bag, actually a wormhole. Winky almost tumbled in and was only saved by a quick-thinking Rumple Tweezer, who pulled Winky from the brink of the "Blue Event Horizon" by his lucky charms! On several occasions, Santa himself had to sprinkle a little of the magic dust around the shop floor to keep the Elves on their toes. Winky was kept too busy to try and see Rudolph. It seemed that either Bimbo or Rumple Tweezer always had an eye on him. All that the Elves were constantly talking about was who would ride with Santa this year. Soon Santa would choose the very best Elves to accompany him on his Christmas Eve ride.

Nobody really wanted to go, for it meant a lot of extra work. While the rest of the Elves were at the PAR TAY of the year, the Elves that went with Santa were incredibly busy delivering billions of presents all around the world in one night's time. It might take a month just to recover from it. Yet it was considered an honor, and there was the magic dust, which is why it might take a month to recover, and all those happy children as well. If it got him close to Rudolph, Winky would do almost anything to go with Santa, if only he could!

Finally, the big day arrived; it was the 23rd of December, the day that Santa would announce who his 'helpers' would be this year. Would Santa choose Winky this year? Finally, Santa and Mrs. Kringle entered the shop just as the Elves were packing the last of the presents for all the good girls and boys all over the world. A hush came over all the Elves as Santa cleared his throat and began. His choices for this year were Larry the Dwarf and Rumple Tweezer. Larry the Dwarf was a good choice as Larry was the tallest Elf. Larry was 6 ft 2 in his stocking feet, rather large for an Elf. While Santa wanted the shop steward to work at least one day a year, much to the chagrin of Rumple Tweezer.

The rest of the Elves began to dance and sing the traditional way to show their thanks for not being chosen and the start of a five-day long party that would send most of them to the hospital. All the Elves except the littlest Elf, who was heartbroken. Winky Tinky hung his head and began to shuffle back to his lonely bed. He crossed the compound to the bunkhouse, and by the time he got there, he was already sobbing gently.

Meanwhile, the shop floor has been turned into a party pit out of Dante's Inferno, and Mrs. Kringle has packed and left for three weeks in the Blue Mountains of Jamaica for a tryst with a Rasta man. Someone's found some old Dio and Sabbath discs and is cranking them out at ear-splitting volume. Larry the Dwarf and Rumple Tweezer are drowning their sorrows in a Vat of Donnie P '58. A few members of the pharmacy staff are pouring little bags of magic dust in the punch bowl as the prim and proper Elf sisters Darla and Dora Dumplings take turns sitting atop the office copier machine, making copies of their naked backsides for use later on at the party.

As this was going on, Winky lay in his bunk and cried his little eyes out over Rudolph. All through the night, while the noise level climbed beyond hearing, Winky cried and cried. Then just after dawn, Winky was shocked back to reality by the blaring sirens of an ambulance sleigh. Winky sprang from his bed to see what was the matter and saw the medics carrying what had to be Larry, the Dwarf. Winky ran across the compound dressed in his nightgown to find that Larry had gone to visit Vixen but had gotten into Cupid's stall by mistake, and what remained wasn't much, but he did have a smile on his face. Santa came up dressed in his red delivery suit with a very hung-over Rumple Tweezer in tow and demanded to know what had happened.

When he found out, he shook his head and smiled to himself and wondered who he should choose now that Larry the Dwarf was out of the picture. Just then, Rumple Tweezer whispered something in Santa's ear, and that jolly old Elf laughed out loud and struck Rumple Tweezer on his shoulder, knocking him to the ground. As Santa choked on laughter, he merrily announced that Winky Tinky would take Larry's place!

As Rumple Tweezer got back on his feet and dusted himself off, Santa told Winky to hurry and get dressed as he was going over to hitch up the reindeer, and then they were leaving. As all the Elves cheered, Winky ran as fast as he could back to get dressed while Bimbo led the Congo line of nearly naked Elves out of the cold and back to the party!

Just as Santa had finished sprinkling the reindeer with the "magic dust," Winky joined Rumple Tweezer in the back seat, and they were off. Through the doors of the barn and into the air, up and up they went. Higher and higher until Winky thought he would surely feint. As Santa checked the radar and other instruments, Rumple Tweezer and Winky opened Santa's bag and prepared to give out the toys. "Uh oh," said Santa as he adjusted his instruments. "Oh shit, wouldn't you just know it?" He exclaimed! "The one night of the year I go out, and the entire planet is covered in Fog!" If he only had got that GPS system last year. How could he deliver the presents to all the good boys and girls?

Then he motioned for Rumple Tweezer to get in the front seat. They talked for a moment, and then Rumple Tweezer got in the back seat and told Winky that Santa wanted to talk to him up front.

When Santa told Winky what he wanted him to do, Winky couldn't believe his ears. He nodded a quick affirmation and stood and took all of his clothes off and waited until Santa sprinkled some "magic dust" on his "Tinky Winky!" He then leaped over the windscreen and onto the backs of the closest reindeer. Winky didn't dare look down from 100,000 feet, and he had to hang on tight in the Mach 2 gale he encountered on the backs of the reindeer. But carefully, he leaped from the back of one reindeer to the next until he came at last to Rudolph! He took no time to make all his dreams come true, which caused Rudolph's nose to glow so brightly that Santa and the reindeer could see to deliver all the Christmas presents to all the good boys and girls throughout the world, and Christmas was saved!

PS. Things have quieted down around the North Pole these days. Santa left for Maui until June with the Dumpling sisters. Mrs. Kringle still hasn't come back from Jamaica, and Rudolph and Winky Tinky have a loft in Frisco.

The End